ONE-WAY TICKET

ONE-WAY TICKET

STORIES

ZINOVY

ZINIK

A NEW DIRECTIONS BOOK

This book is published by arrangement with Harbord Publishing Ltd. London.

Library of Congress Cataloging-in-Publication Data
Zinik, Zinoviĭ.
    [Short stories. English. Selections]
    One-way ticket : stories / by Zinovy Zinik.
      p. cm.
    Translated from Russian.
    ISBN 0–8112–1341–2
    1. Zinik, Zinoviĭ—Translations into English. I. Title.
  PG3490.I495A2 1996   96–9568
    891.73'44—dc20   CIP

Manufactured in the United States of America
New Directions Books are printed on acid-free paper.
Published simultaneously in Canada by Penguin Books Canada Limited

Celebrating 60 years of publishing for James Laughlin
by New Directions Publishing Corporation
80 Eighth Avenue, New York 10011

CONTENTS

ONE-WAY TICKET

A TICKET TO SPARE

THE KIEV MILITIAMAN STOOD AND GAWPED. THE SIGHT OF these blacks jiving away shamelessly, these blacks who had gone and sold out to bourgeois decadence and imperialism, filled him with horror. His face beaded with sweat, he was in despair: on the one hand it was just the sort of occasion for calling in the riot squad; on the other, racism was on the rampage "over there" and, as the political instructor had told them at the briefing, jazz was "a freedom-loving form of expression". An expression of total incomprehension was written not just on the faces in the military cordon; I could not believe my eyes, either. Who would have thought we would hear those sounds, see those bodies in the flesh, in broad daylight, in Kiev Stadium? Up there on stage, in person, reproducing his own famous sound, was Duke himself. For heaven only knows how many years his music had cut through the jamming of various foreign "voices", and here he was, a black with a face bleached by years of using good soap, his hair straightened, stalking in front of his buddies who were swinging away on the stage no more than ten meters from where I was sitting. A fat woman, by the look of her the wife of one of the city bosses, leant close to her husband in his sunflower-patterned shirt and whispered in a broad Ukrainian accent: "I can't see, is he black or isn't he? And his hair's curly brown, or ginger is it?"

Her husband's sunflowers heaved as he sighed: "Don't trouble your head, love. Just listen, eh? Listen!" And his double chin wobbled in time to "Caravan". The floor was throbbing with the music, and through it my feet could sense that

1

the gigantic bust of The Leader in the entrance hall down below was also jiggling to the mighty rhythms. I had the feeling that dragging myself all the way from Moscow down here to Kiev was not going to be a complete waste of time.

"Ladies and gentlemen, I love you," Duke spoke the classic words with which he began all his concerts; but it was one thing to know them from hearsay and quite another to see them coming from his own lips. Yes, he loved us, only he didn't say what for. Like Bernard Shaw loved Russia, according to one of my well-read friends, though for all that Shaw did say: "The Russians showed God the door, but he came bouncing back in through the window in the shape of the NKVD." The great Duke Ellington loved the ladies and gentlemen in his Kiev audience as if he hadn't noticed the militiamen and men in plain clothes in a ring around the stadium. As I had squeezed with my ticket through the security cordon, I had seen two cops grab a kid who had tried to slip past and hustle him away to a car. They weren't beating him up, not as far as you could see, but he was letting out this horrible squeal from having his fingers twisted—discreetly. So, everyone who made it into the concert gripped his ticket in his hot, sweaty fist as if it was a passport to another world, a visa to freedom. For me the irony was that I'd been given my ticket by a friend who'd just been refused a visa to his chosen freedom, Jerusalem, and who had now taken to observing the Sabbath and wearing a black beret. (In Moscow proper skullcaps were hard to find, and in any case attracted too much attention.) There was a time when both of us had been greedy for the forbidden fruit of jazz, and we had equated the freedom of the music-making with freedom of speech. But by the time Duke came to Kiev for that concert in the 1970s, my friend had arrived at a different concept of freedom. "For blacks jazz is the lost motherland. For me Judaism is the jazz the Jews have found," he told me. And when someone in Kiev sent him a ticket for this performance of the blacks' lost motherland, he preferred to stay in Moscow and join a hunger strike in support of the jazz the Jews had found. I didn't argue. I accepted the ticket which no ordinary Muscovite had any hope of obtaining, and I gave thanks in my heart to Judaism, or at least to the hunger strike in its support.

At first the great Duke, whom we had idolized from a distance as a prayer, a hymn and a classic, seemed in the flesh like a cheap jester. What did he think he was doing? Clowning around in drainpipe trousers, a posturing poseur. But his over-familiarity was that of the well-practised clown, being chummy with the audience was part of the job; all that free improvisation, all that jazz without those hateful music stands was an act. This much was clear: if the trombonist, say, were to fluff a single note, a drumstick would come whacking down on his head and the bassist would slice him in half with his bow. And if my friend was right about a motherland lost and jazz gained, then religion and destiny also turned out to be a well-rehearsed circus routine. To the man in the audience truth seems like a circus trick performed by somebody in a black top hat; the clown, though, knows that any trick depends on rules, on discipline, on sleight of hand—and that there can be no question of cheating.

Rationalizing *post factum,* the tricks were being performed on me, though at the time I believed I was a spectator, as I watched Duke prancing, but still I sympathized, hypocritically, with starving Judaism; in this arena, wholly inappropriate for circus stunts, stuffed as it was with militiamen and the overheated wives of Party functionaries, with the plaster bust of the macabre fantast shaking in the entrance, the great bandleader performed acrobatic miracles. The tighter the musicians he held in his power wound our nerves up with the music, the more this ringmaster acted as though nothing special was happening. He created a spectacle out of thin air, producing sounds the way a conjurer pulls a flood of streamers out of an empty top hat. He wandered absent-mindedly across the stage and then, as if he had suddenly remembered an old joke, he fetched a rattle from one corner, wound it pensively, like a clockwork toy, so it made an ironic "trr-rr-rr-i-k-k-k" in the pause that instantly intruded. Or he paced in circles twisting an ordinary jam jar filled with pebbles, and these pebbles made a shooshing noise like shingle in the waves, free and easy among the rumble of artillery fire. Then, while the bass and drums were working themselves and their audience into a frenzy, flailing wildly in a cage of four notes, he squatted down on his haunches and began tapping away at a pair of bongos, as a man waiting for service in a restaurant taps on the table.

Then the music changed: Duke's famous trumpet-solo player picked up his golden horn and pressed his lips to the mouthpiece. All of a sudden his cheeks puffed out from ear to ear like two balloons that made him soar with music, the wrinkles on his forehead giving him a slightly puzzled look.

The trumpet stuck out like a giant cigarette and its full, generous sound was like a welcoming wave of the hand, high above and far away: yes, of course, everything will be fine if you pretend everything is fine and allow yourself the occasional grumble and even the odd tear. Over the course of half an hour these heartfelt appeals built, then suddenly he stumbled on something he seemed never to have encountered before, and it wasn't at all clear how he was going to get himself out of this tangled dialogue with himself, a dialogue he had driven himself into by his own witty calls. Forced as he now was to come up with responses that were no less slick, he puffed out his cheeks and matched every chuckle in the top register with melancholy irony in the bottom one. He faltered, then stopped altogether. Without raising his eyes, as though ashamed of having given in, he took the trumpet from his lips, wiped the sweat from his face and growled into the micro-phone: "Only cats dig me is Jews. Slavery in Egypt!" He waited a second before rounding off this carefully rehearsed aside with a final blare on his trumpet. The stadium erupted; whistles from the veteran jazz buffs and applause from the novices who didn't know you're supposed to stomp your feet when the jazz gets to you, not clap your hands. But neither the veterans nor the novices had really followed what, in actual fact, the trumpeter had growled into the microphone; yet I had heard this remark, which slipped out so easily back in the Bible Belt, on records, and I relished the thought of how I would go back to Moscow and, oh so cool, tell how this American black had made a complaint that would have rocked the Kiev audience if they had only understood it.

Later, when my Kiev nightmare was over, I remembered this remark in the stillness of the hushed stadium as the first, if veiled, hint of the events which would soon develop at break-neck speed. But at the time, during the concert, I noticed only that, while the applause thundered on, a plain-clothes man standing in the gangway bent towards a cop and whispered something in his ear. The cop frowned and went scarlet. Sur-prisingly, though, it was an initiative from the over-excited masses which finished off these provocative forms of expres-sion. During the interval an usherette came out into the gang-way with a stack of programs for sale. This was a fatal mis-take, and even putting a cop to stand next to her was no help: there was a rush for the program with the souvenir photo, everybody was desperate to lay hands on tangible proof of having been in that other world of hitherto-unknown free-dom. First the crowd from the lower rows of seats made a rush at the usherette for these precious programs. Those who couldn't push through began to go round the back via the next gangway, through the foyer, out and then back down the steps from above; sunflower bald spots tangled with sunflowers on bosoms. I watched in despair as my hopes of hearing out this music were smashed into splinters along with the rows of seating. These people had taken freedom literally: they felt everybody had the right to participate in the conjuring trick and that the golden trumpet on the front of the program should be common property, seeing as its music called for universal love. I was one of the first to realize the game was up and it was time to leg it before they decided to break mine for me—you could hear the scrunch of benches and skulls from the gangway and the police cars waiting out in the square in front of the stadium. In jazz I prefer the pauses.

After all that racket, the normal rumble of the city seemed just like one of those wonderful pauses. But not for long. I stood in the square a moment, all wound up, wild, then turned blindly down a side street. Feeling that it was I myself who had gone and got me thrown out on my ears, I tried not to look in people's faces. Because I had gone to the concert straight from the train, I felt as though I were still in a station and I kept imagining those penetrating smells of garlic sausage and hard-boiled eggs that always go with station life. To me the passers-by looked like the crowds of country folk at Moscow stations, armed with string bags and out to raid the food shops. "Hayseeds," I thought, glancing at them furtively hurrying God knew where, until I suddenly remembered I wasn't in Moscow. This was Kiev and I couldn't expect to see the familiar old faces. It wasn't a station crowd I was surrounded by, just ugly mugs, the ones which had haunted Gogol, who hailed from these parts. True, for him the whole of Russia was something out of a nightmare, was one big ugly mug. But then I'm not Gogol and I just wanted to be back in Moscow, away from the faces of this city, the city of Gogol's evil, subterranean goblin, Viy. What I meant by a familiar face is hard to say. Anybody whose eyes signaled "one of us", I suppose.

I studied the neighborhood with annoyance, trying to detect in the buildings some reflection of the warmth I failed to find in people's faces. The shop signs, all in Ukrainian, irritated the eye with their stupid incomprehensible familiarity— the similarity between Russian and Ukrainian, like that between man and ape, one which serves only to emphasize the differences between them and will prevent any kind of merger, because each of them will always insist that the other comes lower on the Darwinian scale.

Every so often the one face I did know in this city swam into view on a poster stuck up on a wall of one of the buildings, which in the luxurious autumn sunlight resembled stale, or maybe overdone, cakes: the face of the great Duke Ellington. It was a three-tier poster in Russian, Ukrainian and English, urging people with triple insistence to go to an event that was over already and merely teased the memory with that heavenly sound, all the more unreal now for having been drowned out by the cracking of bones and the screech of police whistles. I dropped into a post office and tried to scribble a card to Moscow using the words that had flashed across my mind during the performance. I gave up in the end and tore the picture postcard into tiny pieces.

I had to hang around for a train until the following morning, but had absolutely no inclination to go back to where I was staying, which was more of a hostel or communal flophouse than a hotel. It would have been rather like the philosopher Khoma Brut in that Gogol story going back to the chapel to confront Viy at the coffin of the old witch. The hotel was the sort of place where the Soviet traveling factory rep, stripped to his undershirt and suspenders, stuffing himself with pilchards to go with his favorite fruit-and-berry wine, stares at you with sleepy eyes and belches: "Shut the window would you, Comrade. Drafty." Unnerved by the free-for-all at the stadium, I had fled of my own free will from the second half of the freedom I was always going on about. And I could hear the voice of the good Soviet boy scout that had been lurking in my soul since childhood ask the embarrassing question: "How are you going to be able to look your comrades in the eye?" This trip wasn't going to end up as material for a hilariously funny story for me to peddle in Moscow, a story I'd begun working on while still on the train to Kiev. But what was I supposed to do in this city until morning? By this time I had wandered down the steep hill to the old low-lying suburb of Podol, the Dnieper gleaming in the still weather, and lost myself in the maze of narrow streets. I was limping now, my heel rubbed raw. It felt as if every step I took rocked this enchanted city: ripe chestnut conkers hurtled down through the golden foliage overhead and landed on the asphalt with a noise like cracking knuckles, bouncing up and away to one side as if aimed at my back.

My throat was parched from all the walking and I turned down the steps of a basement bar I happened on. It was cool down there, empty and shadowy, and the air held the acid tang of wine from the barrel. I downed a tumbler of dry sherry in one gulp at the zinc-topped counter, wiped my lips and was on my way to the door when I saw somebody beckoning to me out of the semi-darkness of one corner. "Oi, balabosse. C'mover'ere, boss!" What were they calling me for? It was crazy, but it was obviously me they wanted because there was nobody else in the place, except the barmaid, and she'd vanished behind a curtain. In the corner two Kievites, bottle in hand, were sizing me up. Both looked completely out of place in best black suits and ties, in white sweat-stained shirts, frayed at the collar. By the look of them they'd either been to a funeral, a wedding or a Party meeting, all of which amount to much the same in the end.

"They look flashy enough, but they sure do pinch!" One of them was pulling a face as he inspected his gleaming new shoes. He muttered something about having to be off home to the missus and it was obvious that this wasn't the first time he had said it. His comrade, who had meanwhile splashed a generous measure of sherry into my tumbler, retorted that it was in the nature of things for a new boot to pinch, and if your foot felt comfortable it, the boot wouldn't be new any more, would it, and the same, as it happened, went for a woman. Now his old granddad had made him a present of his pocket watch, but he hadn't heard a tick out of it for days. His granddad had given him this gold watch to remember him by, so his granddad's memory wasn't ticking right, not that he was complaining. He held the gold watch to his comrade's ear: "Can you hear it? What did I tell you? And you go on about boots!" Evidently they wanted me to arbitrate between new shoes and granddad's watch. We clinked glasses.

"You from Moscow? Another stinking Muscovite? Have a drink!" said the separatist with the gold watch. "We're not long back from Moscow ourselves. Big place, Moscow. But you'll never find sherry like this there, eh?" He frowned at his glass.

His comrade with the new shoes backed him up: "It's a fact. No sherry." He shook his head. "I was reading in a book by one of them banned Rooshian writers, no sherry in their station buffets. There's cows' udders they say, but sherry's off. Stuff cows' udders, I say!"

The separatist with his grandfather's watch fueled the flames by pouring more sherry: 'What was it one of them bloody Rooshian poets said, that one they were always ramming down your throat at school—Pooshkin: 'What udder name means aught to you!' So, you stinking Muscovite, wha's your name?" Every gesture could have finished either with them cracking me over the head with a glass or inviting me to drink up. They weren't so much unsophisticated as plain drunk.

"Zinovy." I gave my name with some trepidation.

"Wha', wha'?" the owner of the watch demanded with a hiccup. "Nor they can't mend a watch properly in Moscow." He had changed tack. "I went to get my watch fixed in that village of yours. It doesn't tick any more, I said. And the watchmaker, y'know, did he ever have a schnozz and a half—what was it you said your name was?"

I repeated it.

"Well then," he put himself back on course, "there he was sitting there, the ugliest-looking watchmaker you ever set eyes on!" He shook his head.

"Moscow!" began the one with the tight shoes. "I ask this bloke behind the counter: will they be too tight or not? You should've seen his honker. What did you say you were called?" He turned to me.

"Zinovy," I repeated.

"An ugly-looking bugger, but what do you expect?" he concluded with a sigh.

They could not stop harping on about the size of the watchmaker's and the shoe salesman's noses, and when they asked me my name a fourth time, I followed the promptings of cowardice and blurted: "It's a Polish name, by the way."

They both hooted with derision and even seemed to sober up a bit: "Polish? Zinovy! Oh yes, very Polish! You've a lot to thank your parents for, giving you that very Polish name," and they shook their heads and guffawed. "Polish, he says, Polish!"

But I kept my head and asked slyly, weren't they proud of their national hero Bogdan Khmelnitsky? And didn't they know that Khmelnitsky had another name besides Bogdan—Zinovy Bogdan Khmelnitsky. "Check in the Soviet calendar." I downed what remained of the sherry in my glass in triumph. I said I had been born on the same day as the great Ukrainian patriot, the architect of the Ukraine's reunification with

Russia, and my parents, both strong internationalists, had called me Zinovy in honour of Khmelnitsky.

Perhaps the two Kievites really weren't too sure about these details, because they both sat staring at me with their mouths open. But it was more likely that I hadn't thought through exactly what sort of an independent Ukraine they stood for, and whether it was the sort for which Bogdan Khmelnitsky had sold out to Russian autocracy. Because they gulped in surprise and then bore down on me together: "Don't think we don't know what you are. It's as plain as the nose on your face. But you and your kind make out all of us look the same—seen one, seen us all. So you get back to them, go on, git!" They both stood and advanced on me.

"Where to?" I was on my way to the door.

"Over the road. You blind as well as thick? Get over that road."

I shot outside and scurried along the pavement, keeping a sharp lookout over my shoulder. The two separatists stood outside the bar waving their fists, either threatening me or showing me which way to go. I crossed the street, followed a high stone wall, and turned a corner into a dead end. I stopped, not knowing what to do next. The cul-de-sac was deserted, overhung with golden, dust-powdered branches, and seemingly uninhabited. Not one window looked down on you in this useless appendix of the city, a blind gut. The heel of my shoe held my chafed foot in an iron grip. I had no desire to go back out into the street and perhaps have to face the two black-suited separatists. In a lather of panic, as always when compelled to knock at some unfamiliar door, I walked up to a pair of iron gates layered with dusty paint, in an attempt to find a yard or some other way out of the dead end. A breeze stirred and once again I felt myself under fire from the chestnuts that came thudding down on to the asphalt. I leant my head against the metal of the gates, as if shielding myself against this vicious yet impotent hail, and as I waited for an end to the plocking and the scritching of the conkers, which came flying out of their splitting shells as they fell, I unconsciously pressed my hand into some embossed metal ornamentation. Suddenly I felt myself falling forwards; part of the gate, the part I'd been leaning on, turned out to be a little door and had swung open. Barely managing to keep on my feet, I stumbled into a yard and almost fell to my knees in front of a man who was sitting on a bench right beside the gates. The iron door slammed shut on its powerful spring.

The man, dressed in an unseasonable black raincoat, did not get up. He raised his black hat, adjusted his glasses and asked: "Where you from?"

"I'm lost," I said.

"You're not from Kiev? Then what for you are in Kiev?" He shrugged, irritated. "Maybe you should have your eyes tested? Don't you see the posters on every corner? Up in black and white, in three languages: Russian, Ukrainian," he folded down his fingers, "and in German. Perhaps the young man can't read?"

"It's English on the poster, not German. Russian, Ukrainian and a bit in English." I corrected him mechanically, looking round the courtyard, which had a forbidding padlocked building at the far end.

"English?" The man in the hat grinned. "Does it really matter? Today in German, tomorrow in English: report to the crossroads by the cemetery, have your identity papers with you, your money, valuables, also warm clothing, otherwise you are liable to be shot. Or perhaps the young man is a goy?" He lifted his spectacles, the better to study me. "How did you get here on this day of sorrow?"

"By accident," I mumbled.

12

"Nobody gets here by accident," he said as he watched the evening breeze scatter the conker shells.

I tried to think of an excuse to get away. "I'm looking for a chemist. Is there one near here?" I asked, suddenly mindful of my chafed heel. "My foot's sore. I need a bandaid," I continued, for added conviction.

"There is a chemist. Round the corner to the right is an excellent chemist's." Once again he shrugged his shoulders. "But what for you need a bandaid? A bandaid will be no help in the next world."

I made a clumsy bow and tried to retreat backwards to the iron door. After it had clanged shut behind me with a screech of its spring, my eyes resolved its metal ornamentation into a Star of David: the yard, then, belonged to the local synagogue. The neighborhood madman noticed neither my bow nor the slamming of the metal door; he was absorbed in contemplation of a conker shell which had landed at his feet.

The day which had begun with such a swing, with driving rhythms and blaring trumpets, was ending in nightmare. I bit my lip as I walked, either because I felt I had been somehow insulted or because of the pain I was in. I tried not to put any weight on my sore heel, tried not to glance at the bar on my left, turned right then right again at the first corner, as the madman had told me. The street dropped away in front of me, down towards the Dnieper. It was lined with houses, chipped and pockmarked like battered old suitcases. Their shadows lengthened in the evening sun, as though these were giant suitcases being carried downhill by unseen travelers, a living queue jostling towards nobody knew what. And I hurried on down after them.

On the first corner a man in a white chemist's smock stood under a shop sign, *Chemist,* as if expecting me. He was smoking a cigarette, staring into the distance after the shadows as they crept down the slope. He was watching the sunset and smoking, something that these days happens only in Southern towns where people have not forgotten how, come evening, to say farewell to the day. I waited some distance away on the edge of the pavement, trying to decide whether to interrupt his contemplation of the setting sun, spinning in a dusty, golden haze at the bottom of the street. He finished his cigarette, ground it out against his heel, and threw the butt down a grating. He turned to me and asked abruptly: "Can I help?" The huge length of his shadow was scarcely an exaggeration for he was, indeed, immensely tall. I hardly came up to his shoulder. He looked me up and down, and he didn't peer short-sightedly and blink the way you'd expect a chemist to. This look was a blast from both barrels of a shotgun.

"I need a bandaid. I'm lost. I've rubbed my heel raw," I said helplessly.

"Don't you know what the time is? I'm closed. Who sent you to me?"

I hadn't realized Kiev chemists required a letter of introduction. I glanced at my watch. It showed a ridiculously early hour, and putting it to my ear I found it had stopped. Watch on the blink, sore heel killing me, the two separatists, one with a broken watch and the other with shoes that pinched, their troubles coincided with mine—this city was bewitched, damn it—all this was like a clenched fist shoving me in the back: "Get back to where you belong!" I plucked up courage: "They sent me here from the synagogue."

"The synagogue?" He hesitated. "Very well. You can have a bandaid," and he began to unlock the shop door.

While he jangled his bunch of keys, I babbled some sort of self-justification, the way everybody in the Soviet Union does to shopkeepers. "I was at the jazz concert today, utter shambles, the whole thing fell apart, barely managed to get out in one piece, then I went and rubbed my heel raw wandering around Kiev."

When he heard the word "jazz", the chemist turned and looked intently at me again. His eyes combed the street, then suddenly he bent and asked, in a whisper this time: "You from Moscow?"

I nodded, mesmerized by this performance. He said no more, threw open the shop door and pushed me inside. His supercilious aloofness had vanished. He snapped the lock shut and hurried behind the counter, where he began rummaging among packages and boxes. He found something, looked at me again, and repeated his previous question: "From Moscow? A bandaid?"

I smiled guiltily, as if by chafing my heel I had committed an unpardonable error, a mortal sin. I tried to meet his searching gaze, then took to studying my own reflection in the glass-fronted cupboards full of phials, jars and, on one shelf, a mountain of spectacles, or rather of empty frames without lenses, as if they had been stripped from the dead for salvage.

"Here we are. Your bandaid." He placed it on the counter. "Nothing else? You're sure?"

After a day like this one I wasn't sure about anything. My head was throbbing after the sherry, my mouth tasted as though somebody had given me a good punch in the teeth. I remembered I'd forgotten to bring toothpaste with me. "You wouldn't have any toothpaste?" I asked hesitantly.

His lips parted in an unexpectedly cordial smile. For some reason my request made him terribly happy. "Toothpaste? Of course! Why didn't you ask before?" He rummaged behind the counter again. "Which kind of toothpaste? Which sort do you prefer?"

His enthusiasm struck me as rather absurd and I said I really didn't care which kind. Everything about this chemist's struck me as absurd. Actually, this was the very first time I had ever been inside a shop after hours, i.e., face to face, alone with a shopkeeper in an empty shop. The back of my head felt the door lock shut behind me. "I'm really not bothered," I said again, my thoughts returning to toothpaste.

"What do you mean, not bothered?" the chemist fussed. "You've come all the way from Moscow. You are from Moscow, aren't you?"

I nodded. "Oh, all right then. Peppermint will be fine."

This conversation was beginning to sound like something out of a spy story. It was obvious he was interested in a lot more than he dared say. "I don't have change, you realize. I've closed out the register already," the chemist said before I had produced even a kopeck out of my pocket. It struck me he might be trying to squeeze some extra money out of me, a desperate passing customer. All I wanted to do was sit down, anywhere, then and there, or best of all lie down—even that hotel would have done—lie down with a blanket pulled up over my head and shut out this city. I certainly didn't want to start arguing, so I put my hand in my pocket and, ignoring all the change I had which would have been enough for a dozen bandaids, produced a ruble note.

The chemist grabbed it and began waving it about. "For you, though, I will try and find change. Let's go." He took my elbow and guided me to the back door. His grip on my arm was firm: resistance would have been useless. On the other side of the door a narrow staircase led downwards and a dim light burned at the foot. I was marched down.

I tried to protest: "What are you doing to me?"

The chemist only whispered: "Ssshh! Just one more step now!"

Filtering out through a crack of light I heard a plangent sound, either of weeping or singing, as unsettling as a premonition of the future. A door was thrown open. After the gloom of the staircase, the light in this room was dazzling. Twelve men were seated around a long table. They all seemed very much alike, the way a row of Party functionaries sometimes will, sitting, arms folded, on the platform. As my eyes gradually grew accustomed to the light, I was able to make out the points of similarity between the members of this conclave: every single one of them was wearing a black skullcap or beret. Each had a dog-eared volume lying open in front of him. The table, spread with a white cloth, was dominated by two objects—an uncorked bottle of deep-red wine and a seven-branched candlestick. Now I knew where I was. I was among the Jews.

"The man from Moscow." The chemist pushed me forward. I stood there blinking in the light. All twelve covered heads swiveled slowly towards me. The last to do so belonged to the man sitting at the head of the table with his back to me. I expected to see a grey beard and bushy eyebrows. But the face that stared at me was hard and youthful, younger than any of the others there, one of those bold, reckless faces I had seen in the company of my Moscow friend. He looked at me in absolute silence, then turned to the chemist and said in a light dry tenor: "Not him." And the twelve all went back to their books again and once more took up their mumbling— was it wailing or chanting? As far as they were concerned I no longer existed. But I knew I was among my own; that they were gathered here in secret; that they were expecting somebody, an emissary from Moscow; that I wasn't him. I wasn't the emissary. But I did know what was going on. Perhaps I had made my exodus from the second half of the blacks' lost motherland only to finish up in the jazz the Jews had found. I could tell them about all the people who might be their emissary, I could come up with the phrase I had picked up from my friend, *aleikum salaam*, I was well up in these things: Zion, the sabbath, and keep off the salami. But I didn't say *salaam* to the leader of the Jews for confiding in me, a Prodigal Son. I'd lost my nerve and had a suspicion that after the fatal words "not him", the interpretation the chemist and the others of the twelve would put on every step I had taken on the way to that brightly lit room was that I was a snitch and a double-dealer. And anything I might say about my belonging to the chosen people too would only go to prove it. The chemist began shoving me towards the door. At the top of the stairs, before he finally sent me packing, he dug a heap of coins out of his pocket and forced them into my hand: "Your change! Your change!"

I was standing in the dark in a strange city, the conkers thudding down, with a defunct watch and a very sore heel, with a filthy taste in my mouth which didn't go away until I reached Moscow, where I was drily informed that I had been in Kiev on the anniversary of the slaughter of the Jews, on the day prayers were held in secret for the victims of Babi Yar.

But I, a person who has always been received by everybody, everywhere, on every occasion, had had the door of the one place in the world I most wanted to be in at that particular moment slammed shut without ceremony in my face. Looking back there is just one thing I want to find out: who was it those men were expecting in that Kiev basement? I know for sure it was not my friend, who might have found himself in my shoes had he not given me that ticket which happened to be spare.

1980

Translated by Frank Williams

THE REFUGEE

VIENNA SEETHED WITH FORMER SOVIET CITIZENS. IN THOSE years that town of eternal spies and former Nazis, with a third man around every corner, was still a staging post for emigrants leaving the Soviet Union—with fictitious invitations from fictitious uncles and grandmothers—on the pretext of family reunification. It was one such great nephew from Moscow that I had come there' to meet. Like everything connected with Moscow departures, my friend's telegram was a mixture of idiocy, tactlessness, and a naive, adolescent egotism: "Arriving Vienna first week of May meet me yours Rabinovich." You can well imagine how many Soviet Rabinoviches passed through Vienna in those years, and in this sense the first week of May 1979 was not particularly remarkable. But my Rabinovich naturally considered himself an exception to the rule. Furthermore, he obviously supposed that Vienna was only a few streetcar stops from London; he was therefore clearly convinced that there were streetcars in London—if there are streetcars in Moscow, how could there not be in London? The Vienna streetcars did impress me—their appearance, their chimes, the very rails led back to Moscow.

There were, roughly speaking, two varieties of Rabinoviches arriving from Moscow. Those bound for Israel immediately left for a town house with a red cross on the roof that masked the stars of David on their chests, and from there to Tel Aviv. Those headed for America, or trying to get a foothold somewhere in Europe, received the status of political refugees. Different types of charitable organizations (depend-

19

ing on the country of destination) took them under their wings: they doled out a miserly stipend and moved them to bed and breakfasts and cheap hotels while their immigration papers were being processed. Since I knew neither the exact date of arrival, nor my Rabinovich's ideologico-geographical intentions, I had no choice but to search for him along several lines simultaneously. In short—a lost cause. But there was no way out of it.

I felt beholden. In the months before my departure Mark and I had grown fairly close. However, the words "grown close" must be understood in the narrow, Muscovite, Soviet sense. Mark Rabinovich was one of the "farewell activists" of the emigration era; at that time no farewell parties took place without him. He personally assumed all the trouble of filling out forms, getting permission to export books or paintings, and he saw to the expedition of trunks and the disposition of apartments. Due to the lack of commercial companies and paid servants our household tasks were solved with the help of friends; household fuss and bother was therefore seen as a kind of intense form of friendship, and the overcoming of household crises and squabbles as the apogee of intimacy. In any event, Mark Rabinovich, at one time an active participant in the bustle surrounding my departure from Moscow, now considered me virtually his closest friend "beyond the cordon". It was my turn to play a role in his destiny—if not with friendship, then at least with a reciprocal bustle around his arrival in Vienna.

Since I had dual citizenship—Israeli and British—connections were immediately established with all of the immigration agencies, émigré organizations and diplomatic services; as a result not a day passed without a phone call to my hotel informing me of the arrival of yet another Mark Rabinovich. The fact that he wasn't from Moscow, wasn't the right age, wasn't a redhead, and indeed wasn't the correct

Rabinovich in any respect, was always discovered at the last moment. I obediently trudged off to each and every center, pension, hotel, and charitable organization in order to encounter yet another oddity of emigrant fate—hysterics, chaos, terror, and the scandalous extortion of spongers.

I saw two retirees, former Honored Bolsheviks, their false teeth falling out, spitting at each other, teeth, slobber, and all. They were arguing in hoarse voices: was it or was it not possible in the state of Texas to arrange for a subscription to the Soviet magazine *The Worker's Wife* to be delivered to your home?

I saw Jews who spent days sewing all their personal belongings, including aluminum saucepans, into the linings of their jackets. They were preparing for illegal entry into West Germany under train wagons and in the trunks of cars; in West Germany, rumor had it, Jews were given honorary citizenship and financial compensation for the horrors of Nazism.

I saw people who were firmly convinced that the goal of the Israeli immigration agencies was to kidnap them from their hotel and, under the watchful eyes of German shepherds and the muzzles of Uzis, to sent them off to forced labor in the socialist kibbutzes of the Negev desert.

I saw people who filled suitcase after suitcase with plastic shopping bags; in Vienna this was the most available symbol of prosperity for those guided by Soviet criteria. The plastic rubbish bags handed out to the guests by the hotel administration were also stashed away. These shiny bags were stored away in the treasure chest of future well-being, and at night the rubbish was furtively thrown into the hall or through the windows onto the street. The halls reeked with the refuse of the Soviet past.

The plumbing no longer worked in most of the hotels. It was clogged, primarily by newspapers: following long-standing Soviet habit, newspapers were used in lieu of toilet paper, and the toilet paper was stashed away and then sold at improvised émigré flea markets. But worst of all were the chicken feathers flushed down the toilets. Former Soviet citizens, landing in Vienna like hens for the plucking, had quickly figured out that the cheapest meat product in the West was chicken. In Russian logic, chicken that had been drawn, cleaned, and packed in shiny plastic wrapping with a supermarket label should cost considerably more than chicken sold in the markets in its "wild" condition. The émigrés bought live birds at market, slaughtering and disembowelling them in their hotel rooms. The plucked bird was thrown into the Rainbow-brand electric pot, and the feathers were flushed down the lavatory. That is, the feathers didn't flush at all, the pipes were already stuffed with the feathers of previous chickens.

These hotels for Soviet émigrés were recognizable at a distance by the stench, and also by the constant commotion and crowds of various species of humanity around the entrance. There was inevitably an archetypally lanky tough in a T-shirt with a dim-witted expression on his face who loitered there all day as if in front of a brothel. His air of businesslike preoccupation manifested itself only in the incessant working of his jaws: they zealously masticated chewing gum, a shortage item finally acquired in unlimited quantities. Old ladies in those familiar scarves always gossiped there, settling themselves, in the absence of a bench, directly on the steps or on beer cases. Against the magnificent, May-time cream-cake of Vienna, drowning in spring waltzes and young wine, these émigré dormitories—cans of worms clamoring with the congested humdrum of life—looked like leper colonies, like a plague quarantine.

After unmasking yet another false Rabinovich, I fled this émigré contagion to Grinzing, a Vienna suburb an hour's streetcar ride from the center. The bucolic sight of cob-blestoned lanes, where every house had a gingerbread roof, a wine cellar, and tables in the courtyard, where housewives in peasant headdress and crinolines with aprons over lace pet-ticoats carried mugs brimming with young wine—all of this seemed disdainfully to avoid those slovenly layabouts and the crowded Vienna neighborhoods, so urbanely indiscriminate in their readiness to shelter aliens such as my kinsmen in emigration, with their suitcase hubbub, sweaty paws, and ob-noxious tenacity. During those days in Vienna I myself devel-oped with frightening facility that instinctive condescension and scorn, the grimace of impenetrability when you ignore a poor relation or a superfluous, down-and-out old friend at a social gathering, that badly-brought-up aristocrat's habit of jerking a shoulder and walking by without so much as a turn of the head. However you looked at it, I considered my-self an aristocrat of the emigration, while they—new Soviet arrivals—were its plebeians, its *lumpen proletariat*.

Avoiding contact with them wasn't hard at all: they were visible a mile away, like a pimple on the cleanly-shaven chin of Vienna. Something inexplicably Soviet could be immediately detected in the sadly bowed, bull-like necks, in the mindless purposefulness of their walk (in search of shortages?), in the submissively hunched backs and lowered faces gazing up from below the brow. Or, on the contrary, in the doltishness of the open mouth and eyes sticking out for joy, in the nasal, hysteri-cal voice, commenting indiscriminately and incessantly on ev-erything, like a village bard in a teahouse. There was some-thing in the exaggerated gesticulation, as if these hands, longing for possessions, wanted to fondle everything in this new world of dreams-come-true. It was precisely to this sec-ond category that the man who sat down opposite me on the square at the streetcar stop belonged. I was waiting for the streetcar back to Vienna after one of my Grinzing bouts.

Slightly tipsy, I had missed one streetcar. The next was in half an hour; there was nothing left to do but sit down on the bench and observe, hiding myself for appearance's sake behind a newspaper, the classic pantomine of emigration's grimace.

He wasn't alone. Vehemently gesticulating and swaying talmudically, he was expounding his authoritative opinion—undoubtedly on topical questions of world politics and the fate of civilizations—to a portly American woman in a summer panama and a severe, polka-dotted dress. She was clearly one of those charitable ladies, volunteers from American agencies that take care of Soviet Jews arriving in Vienna as if they were mentally ill relatives. Indeed, the impression my compatriot made was not entirely normal. He was about fifty years old, and one of that appalling breed of debaters from the provincial intelligentsia—perhaps an engineer, or a history teacher disillusioned with Marxism-Leninism. Everything about him spelled a half-educated demagogue from the Russian sticks: stocky and swollen like a homely potato, not in height but in width, he was corseted by an over-washed cowboy shirt that clung to him like a fruit rind. His skin, dusty with sunburn, contrasted with the grizzle of his road-worn unshavenness; the apparently broken frames of his eyeglasses were bound near the ear-piece with adhesive tape and he held them delicately with two fingers in an unexpectedly parodical, professorial gesture.

Mechanically skimming the newspaper page I shuddered, as if caught red-handed, from the hard, rolled Russian "r" in the unthinkable, broken, dismembered English of my former compatriot. Apparently I was the only one in the vicinity capable of guessing the meaning of his sentences, which he shouted in a strained voice straight into the American woman's ear. As might have been expected, it amounted to condemning the Austrian population for its lack of human warmth and insufficient opposition to Soviet infiltration of the Near East. Every Soviet person knew precisely on whom an atom bomb should be dropped in order to save everything lofty and humanitarian on this earth. Tolerance consisted of dropping the bomb on some immediately and on others a bit later; differences of opinion arose only on the issue of timing.

These strategic subtleties obviously interested the American lady only because my former compatriot was under her care and administrative supervision. She nodded readily in agreement, but her gaze wandered lazily about the square: it was the look of nurses assigned to patients in private psychiatric clinics. When her dogged interlocutor began to wave his arms about too violently, I could hear her polite, noncommittal objections. That's how one talks with people who cannot be held accountable for their actions. In any event, the conversation changed course. The American woman rose and, energetically shaking hands with my truth-seeker, strode off, with the enviable joviality of portly people, in the direction of the wine cellars, from whence bold singing could already be heard, accompanied by the clink of mugs, as if in imitation of the classic sound track of Soviet films on Nazi debauchery. A camera hung from the American woman's shoulder and I thought that perhaps she wasn't in charge of my former compatriot after all, but had run into him accidentally, started up a conversation with him by chance. Without caretakers or debating opponents this type clearly could not exist: the American woman had only to walk off for his eyes to begin combing the square in search of new ideological victims. I immediately plunged even further into my English newspaper.

But it was too late: he was heading implacably in my direction, and in a moment had already sat down on the other end of my bench. Looking around, he began moving closer in spurts, diminishing the distance between us like a drunken idler trying to pick up a girl on the avenue. Out of the corner of my eye I observed his pantomime of mystifying nods, incoherent ahems, inviting smiles, winks, and jerks until I finally realized that it represented a request for a light. He simply had no matches. Without quite turning around, I retrieved my lighter and brought the flame to the cigarette hanging from his teeth. At the last second a gust of wind swept the lighter flame aside, my uninvited neighbor jerked, the cigarette flew out of his mouth, he grabbed it in flight with his fist, and before our eyes all that remained of the cigarette was a bit of torn paper and a few shreds of tobacco. He immediately began patting his pockets in search of a pack, found a chewed-up paper wrapper—the cheapest local variety—and convinced himself that it was completely empty. His spectacles with their taped earpiece slid down his nose. He looked so entirely pathetic that I couldn't take it and I proffered my packet of Benson and Hedges. He delicately withdrew the cigarette with two fingers, sniffed it, studied the English brand name and said, respectfully, half-enquiringly:

"Inglysh?" No longer doubting, he flicked the *Times* on my lap with his finger: "Inglysh!"

That thin, transparent newspaper, black with foreign letters, that very "inglysh" became for me at that moment a trusty political asylum, a bulletproof glass, behind which I could sit out the émigré attack in complete emotional safety, and at the same time not miss a single facet of the Martian alien's metabolism. To acknowledge my birth meant to erase my own lengthy experience of freedom from the slavery of a Soviet past and once again to associate with the hustle and bustle of the émigré crowd in the choice of a new homeland. Every Rabinovich of this round possessed perfectly indisputable opinions on where it was best to move. Nonetheless, each enthusiastically awaited refutation of his final decision, because he secretly suspected that someone else knew something that he didn't; someone somewhere else is getting something a little better than what we have here. Full of aristocratic disdain for such plebeian dilemmas, I nodded, unblinking, and affirmed that I was indeed "inglysh". If I acknowledged my Russian origins, the conversation would immediately turn to elucidations of where and how it was possible to set yourself up. I wasn't interested in increasing the Russian ethnic minority of the British Isles.

My Rabinovich energetically dragged on the English cigarette, once again straightened the broken earpiece of his eyeglasses with those instructorish two fingers, wiped his chin and, moving over to me in earnest, confidingly informed me in his monstrous English, that he was quite unhappy with England. I expressed cautious interest: in precisely what respects had England failed to satisfy him? England, as it turned out, didn't help Israel. I muttered something about the Balfour declaration and said that even Muslim nations said that Israel was England's creation. To this the implacable Rabinovich objected that English pederasts were known to love Muslims, all of whom should have been castrated long ago; the English placed an embargo on the sale of arms to Israelis, instead of sticking a nice little bomb up the rear end of Palestinian terrorists. These Palestinians, whose balls should have been torn off long ago, had set up shop in Lebanon and gave the local Christian population no peace, but the entire world, with the exception of Israel, shut their eyes to it.

Here my curiosity about the ravings of my former compatriot began to give way to old hostility: once again Russians know whose balls should be torn off and who should be castrated; once again we're surrounded by enemies and the unsightliness and impoverishment of our life and thought is someone else's fault; yet another plot against Christian civilization is being planned and, in order to save it, yet another bomb should be dropped on someone else. Silently I thrust a spread of the

Times under the nose of this justice seeker—a photograph of the latest Israeli bombing of a Palestinian camp near Beirut.

The corpses of old men, women and, naturally, children, and even a terrorist with missing balls in the hospital, were satisfyingly atrocious. My compatriot gazed at this photograph, as if he was transfixed. The papers, radio, and television had been sounding off about this attack for almost a week, but this was the first this Soviet Rabinovich had heard about it.

"In English and Austrian I doesn't understands so good," he admitted, mangling his grammar, and for the first time in the whole conversation an expression of helplessness appeared on his face.

"You could take a look at the Russian paper," I said. "They give the émigré press to you for free in the hotels."

"In what hotel?" he swung his head around. He didn't read Russian. He despised the Russian language. The Soviet Union spoke Russian, and the Soviet Union supported his blood enemies, the Palestinian terrorists.

"And just what language do you read, if not Russian, I'd like to know?" said I, infuriated by this born-again Zionist. "What language did they teach you in school, for heaven's sake? Jewish? Or maybe it was Arabic?"

"Well, yes—Arabic," he nodded. French, and of course Arabic. He was bilingual, like every Lebanese Christian from Beirut. And he gestured with his hands, as if apologizing for knowing Arabic.

The cowboy shirt turned out to be of Lebanese make. As did the filthy trousers with bulges at the knees, and the broken eyeglass frames and the shoes with crepe rubber soles out of season, and the hard, rolled "r" of his pronunciation. His house had been blown up by Palestinians who had seized his block. They had shot his entire family. He had barely had enough for a ticket to Europe. How and why he ended up in

Austria was hard to understand: the route of every emigrant on earth is explainable less by practical geography than by an accounting with the past and hopes for the future, and for each emigrant these are too confused for a chance fellow-traveler to understand.

I only found out that he worked as a dishwasher here and came out during his free time to talk with tourists. Through them he discovered what was happening in the world—he had no money for newspapers, and for that matter he didn't know where the French and Arabic newspapers were sold. He didn't venture out of this suburb, dreamed only of the liberation of his country, and was sometimes visited by vague thoughts of emigrating to America. I was the first person with whom he'd been able to talk seriously about the events in Lebanon. There was nothing left for me to do but to take up the *Times* and read to him everything on the Lebanese situation, explaining unfamiliar words and commenting on the facts. Half an hour later another streetcar passed, but I didn't get up from the bench. My voice already hoarse, I continued to read the English paper from cover to cover to this eccentric Lebanese—until it grew dark.

By way of a postscript: my Muscovite Rabinovich never showed up in Vienna after all; despairing at the wait, I returned to London where I found a telegram from him, informing me that he'd decided against emigrating and had turned down his exit visa.

1987

Translated by Jamey Gambrell

MEA CULPA

AT THE FAR EXTREMITY OF AFRICA NEAREST THE EASTERN Coast of the Mediterranean, the sun, as it sinks into the setting West, obliterates everything in its path, the distance between objects as well. Eliding perspective, the homogeneity of this celestial incandescence makes the white cubes of the hotels look like clouds—though there are none at this time of year—and the whitewashed native shanties look like slightly grubby flecks of foam. People and objects are reduced to their contours, turn into cut-outs, like one of those designs on a kimono transferred to human skin in the radioactive flash of Hiroshima. A palm tree is superimposed on the sea, an orange on a naked breast, the horizon fuses with a beach umbrella. The world is seen as a flat projection, a slide with a blindingly powerful lamp behind the lens. Absence of depth and distance sweeps the nudists scattered along the beach into a single orgiastic heap. In a show of modesty, you retreat beneath an awning, but staying in the shadows makes you a shadier character still. Though coming back out into the sun does nothing to whiten it: you just go pink. And not with embarrassment, either. Such is the moral dialectic of the beach. This is the East, where collectivism rules supreme and your Western individualism is as thin as your return ticket to London. Not that you keep it on you. It's back in your room. Trousers (civilization) and body (nature) are no longer a single entity.

This flatness of landscape and muddling of perspective infect your view of past, present, and future. How lucky the people of the desert, the people of the East are. The uniformity of the horizon means that distance is measured by time, and time by the changing tints of the horizon. Under a sun like that, the whole of existence merges into one long, drawn-out moment. This endlessness and immobility lie at the heart of the East with its enormous optimism so alien to the West's nostalgia for times past and the West's despair, provoked by constant departures, changes of geography, the metamorphosis of the near into the distant and *vice versa*—in short, by a constant sense of loss. The opposite is no less true. No one who feels exalted at the stirring times he has lived through and the distance he has covered can come to terms with the ahistoricity of lazing on the beach in the East, where all go naked before Time, like a nudist under the seaside sun, the medals of a heroic past locked in a strongbox and the keys tossed into the drifting sands.

After soaking up enough solar timelessness, I strolled back from the beach to the town square. Little restaurants and souvenir stands crowded round a concrete apron, ice cream and falafel vendors competed with the wailing pop of the music shops. The locals compensated for the absence of any perceptible temporal or spatial changes by artificially generating noise and movement. The restaurant owners' fussing around their empty tables, their scurrying from the bar to the doorway and back to attract custom, the way they almost dragged their customers in, formed perhaps the only point of similarity between the holidaymakers and the indigenous population. Though even this was an illusion. In their anxiety to turn a profit, the restauranteurs danced rather than scurried about their business. They performed a ritual ballet to lure the clientele, regardless of whether that clientele was in the vicinity or not. The concert went ahead with or without an audience. The tourists surged back and forth across the square, shying nervously away at every move to draw them into one or another establishment, sensing that this ritual native dance in the square had a hidden purpose—to clean

31

them out, rip them off, and possibly poison them into the bargain.

I was sitting one day in my favorite Arab café in a corner of the square, watching as if at the theater these various antics going on and smiling condescendingly the while. It was an unprepossessing place, the tables were plastic and you had to ask specially if you wanted a paper napkin. But the place served a remarkable *hummus* and you couldn't get a better coffee even in East Jerusalem. Its scruffiness—tables spilling out on the street—saved it from being inundated by tourists. I would sit over a coffee, waiting for the newsvendor to open up after the siesta. I'd drop by every day, on my way back from the beach, to pick up a copy of the *Herald Tribune*. In these surroundings the familiar English constructions began to sound incoherent, and gave a weird feeling of pleasure precisely because of that incoherence. Government crises and stock market crashes, political scandals and generation gaps, the right to choose your place of residence and the interconnection of time, civic conscience, and the end of an affair, these were all a mirage—what else could they be in a country of eternally blue skies? They were all as illusory as, say, the diversity of the faces in the crowd I sat watching in the square.

What multifariousness, you might think, what a kaleidoscope of faces, clothes, and behavior. But if you looked closely, you found astonishingly repetitive stereotypes: high cheekbones, thick lips, albino pallor, freckles, and that's it—that exhausted the whole gamut. The extravagant variety of their clothes could quickly be classified by the stripe of the various countries and nationalities. And while it might be hard to assess a person's precise ethnic origin, the passport he held could be guessed at a glance. If not his current one, then his true one, the one he started out with. It crossed my mind I might even see a face horribly reminiscent of Mikhail Sergeyevich Grets. How on earth could they have got here—

those powerful balding temples, etched as if by sweat? Or those uniquely Russian massive lobal bumps, which identify the denizen of Soviet public libraries? Or the broad, stooping, bull-like neck and shoulders that come from years of bending to talk in the library smoking-room, back pressed into a corner, speaking from behind the hand, trying to catch what the other person's saying through the smoke? Or those blatantly Soviet horn-rims that have been slipping down his nose these past forty years, so that the index finger, in forever pushing them back up, has almost grown into his forehead in a gesture of eternal reflection, an everlasting posing of choices?

This type was more of an anthropological specimen, apparently, than a specific socio-historical one. The physiological similarity between Grets and an overweight tourist in a panama hat was astonishing. I had not even completed this formulation in my mind before a completely different thought began to seep through the convolutions of my brain. This type, who had the hunted look of any starving new arrival, was steadily moving in my direction and with every step, with every shuffle of his rubber-soled shoes, a somewhat unexpected conclusion was being beaten into my temples as loudly and strongly as the pounding of my heart. The resemblance between the person approaching me and Mikhail Sergeyevich Grets was not simply surprising—the resemblance between them was perfect, so perfect that this person and Mikhail Sergeyevich Grets were identical. In other words, the person bearing down on me was none other than Mikhail Sergeyevich Grets himself.

In Moscow people of his own generation had been giving him a wide berth as far back as Khrushchev's legendary thaw in the late fifties. He plagued Moscow gatherings during the *samizdat* sixties, forever calling everyone out into the streets to immolate themselves as human torches. In the seventies, he was the one forever denouncing Jewish emigrants as rats leaving a sinking ship. He wanted them to remain, Russian frogs croaking the truth in a Soviet swamp. He didn't so much produce elaborate syllogisms and outmoded paradoxes, as reproduce them. He was a tape machine for recording public opinion, one with a mighty powerful amplifier. He bored his friends by announcing as amazing discoveries things they had learned long ago from bitter personal experience. Callow youths and neurotic adolescents were the only people he could depend on to accept his role as martyr and latter-day Socrates, parroting after him the tired old *samizdat* slogans about crystal palaces built on the blood of infants, revolutionary utopias ending up as totalitarian nightmares, passive silence being no less criminal than active informing. They simply could not remain silent. They were utterly fixated, huddled in conspiratorial knots, while their intolerance was a mirror image of that of the Bolsheviks. I found it all repulsive, which made me an outsider and forced me to adopt a course of resolute isolation.

I knew perfectly well, of course, what Grets meant when he launched into his muddled declarations about being guilty of complicity in the dreadful things that were going on. He belonged to the generation that discovered too late—a century after the event—Dostoyevsky's once-banned novel, *The Possessed*. He was horrified to recognize one of the heroes in himself. Unlike his generation, tainted Dostoyevskian characters that they were, we felt rather like ashamed readers of *The Possessed*. At a certain point, the book became hateful to both groups and we slammed it shut. And so, we had both found ourselves in exile. Though instead of beginning a new life, he embarked on a repeat of the same old story, making new enemies here to keep up the old effort to prove his own rightness back there.

Deliberations on the totalitarian paradise built on the blood of infants and on silence being criminal in that atmosphere of complicity were swapped for a more historiographical version of the old question "Who is to blame?", in an émigré version this time. Had the Bolsheviks landed from Mars in dialectical tripods? Or was Soviet power merely the dialectical consummation of the slavish trinity of Orthodoxy, Autocracy, and People? He felt his departure into emigration was a public protest against Soviet serfdom and regarded all the regime's steps down the road of liberal reform as a threat to his own heroic past, present, and future in emigration. If everything was so liberal over there now, what had been the point in emigrating?

I used to bump into him every so often on the highways and byways of the Russian community abroad: at premieres, conferences, in private homes. Besides, his wife came from a wealthy Greek family which patronized the arts and literature, especially Russian literature. And where money and grants are to be had, people gather. Whenever we met, he would take my arm and pin me in a corner as if we were back in the old library smoking-room, then start interpreting the latest trends in Europe, which proved, in his dazzling exposé, to be nothing less than the same old Bolshevism dressed up in new clothes. I had a vision of his waving as he recognized me, putting his arm round my shoulder, sitting down at my table, leaning towards me earnestly and launching into his latest conspiracy theory, utterly fascinating to him, deadly boring to the rest of us.

The very thought struck me in the temple, pierced the trifacial nerve, and seared my eyeballs like a blinding ray of Mediterranean sun reflected from Grets's horn-rims. My first reaction was to run, and to hell with the bill. But at that moment the crowd parted, as if on purpose, and I sank back into my chair. A corridor cleared between us, four duellists' paces long. A sudden movement and his eye would trap me in the lens of his glasses. And with me this beautiful, sun-drenched world, naive as a primitivist painting. No more the suntanned female knee at the next table, blurring into the pile of oranges on the bar, behind which a swan floated across a tacky reproduction lake, tangling with a white sail out at sea in the corner of the back window. No longer the illusion of leading the simple life far from our apocalyptic tumbles and eschatological leaps. I was only kidding myself. No matter what the sun did here, collapsing human destinies and distances, in this setting a Russian intellectual like Grets (be he Tatar, Yid, or Russian) would be still more clinging, unavoidable, insistent, like the shadow of a cloud sliding over the sun in England. I was pinned by the apex of that shadow to my place at the table, hoping the cloud would slip away over the horizon. If I sat without moving a muscle, the sharp eye of this snake that had come slithering out of the bushes of Russian spirituality might pass over me, this Westernizing rationalist rodent.

But no, the ideologically-sharpened pupils of this Russian bookworm and Pharisee fixed directly on me. I slumped. Like a bed-ridden invalid, I half raised myself, supporting myself on the table with one hand and giving him a feeble, if ostensibly friendly, wave with the other.

No reaction. His beady, unwinking eyes continued to eat me up. Not a muscle moved in his face. He was looking straight at me without, however, seeming to see me. "Maybe he's gone blind these last few years?" In a panic I was trying to remember whether he'd always worn glasses and what kind they were, though at the same time I was well aware that if he was blind he wouldn't need glasses. His hypnotic glare petrified me, literally. Sweat poured down my face. Reproach was written in his silence, in the clenched line of his mouth, and his unwavering stare. It was the wordless reproach of a prophet, that unspoken reproach and disparaging mien of an oracle foretelling world catastrophe, an imminent ice age called totalitarianism, from which ice age I had so heedlessly fled to this tropic clime of flat ideas and uncomplicated journeys. I looked round for what I thought might be the last time, taking in this place which had no real meaning and was, therefore, paradise to me. From the moment Grets appeared on the scene, this uninhabited islet was threatened with transformation into a Soviet communal flat dense with all the usual ideological squabbles.

My eyes lit on a menu hung up behind me in the doorway; I suddenly realized what it was he had been staring at so fixedly. Like in many such small eating places, the menu had been scribbled up on a blackboard. Middle-aged Grets had the look of a schoolboy nailed by the teacher's question to the board on which a classmate has scrawled some obscure formula. He obviously didn't know the answer. The menu was half in Arabic, half in illiterate and spidery English, the prices and dishes all out of sync. I watched Grets move his lips, mouthing repetitively to penetrate the meaning of the hieroglyphs on the board. The greater his concentration on the mysteries of the menu, the more forcibly it came home to me how terribly selective human vision is. It fails to absorb even objects that fall within its field; it obeys the laws of subjective idealism. Man sees only what he wants to see. Mikhail Sergeyevich Grets was horribly hungry. And thus he failed to see even his ideological opponents, myself included. He saw menus, the various menus of the various eating places. For all my variety, I was not on a menu and so he did not see me. He was looking over my head.

Very cautiously, trying not to draw his attention, I slid off my chair and sidled crouching away from the tables. I never for a second took my eyes off Grets. There was only one avenue of retreat, up some stairs to a first floor arcade of shops and restaurants. From this moment my mind was beset by ideological dilemmas. I was thinking like a partisan behind

enemy lines, like a strategist trying to thwart an enemy block-
ade. This gallery served one useful purpose at least. Up there I
had an excellent vantage point on Grets's every move. I pictured myself with a spyglass, following his movements from
eating-place to eating-place, from window to window. Eventually he stopped at a postcard rack outside a café where the
Herald Tribune was usually on sale to an English-speaking
"intellectual" clientele.

He stood there, turning the stand, examining the post-
cards, and I got mad at myself for watching him. Why was I
interrupting my postprandial cup of coffee and perusal of the
IHT for that old fart? Surely I could dig down to that vein of
inner hardness that would deliver me from this hypocrisy and
let me give him the standard brush-off, "lovely to see you, but
some other time perhaps"? Why did I have to hide from him,
like some truant schoolboy hiding from his parents? At that
moment he looked up and scanned the upper story, focusing
for a second, so I thought, on the staircase where I was standing. My knees went wobbly again and my heart sank, like a
schoolboy's heart before exams. Had he spotted me? Surely
not! With his short sight! But why short sight? Why not long?
How did I know? Was I his optician or something?! By now
even madder at myself, and at these existential dilemmas, I
drew myself demonstratively up to full height, held my head
high and clattered loudly down the stairs, only to grab nervously at the handrail and skulk behind the passers-by when I
saw Grets approach the tables of "my" establishment.

Once again he was dumbly examining the unyielding
menu. Then, glancing around furtively in a very Russian manner (in my anxiety, meanwhile, I had dived behind yet another
passing back), he sat down at a table and began mopping the
sweat from his brow. Did this mean he knew a good place
when he saw one? What was it about this place, a place which
hardly looked different from a dozen others, that made him

choose it? The appearance of the place and the dishes displayed in the glass cabinet were more likely to put off a person like Mikhail Sergeyevich Grets, who regardless of climate, craved only his Russian borsch and meat balls with kissel for dessert. The only possible explanation was that he'd seen me sitting there. And since I was a well-known connoisseur of such matters, the fact that I had chosen this establishment meant it must be the place to eat. That was Grets's remorseless logic. Unless, of course, he was guided by some other logic, the logic, for example, of a chance decision.

However it was, he didn't stay there long. Clutching a copy of the *IHT* in my sweaty paw, rather like the proverbial dog with a paper between its teeth, I wove through the crowd to the edge of the magic concrete square that marked the restaurant's territory. Suddenly, a few feet away a face began to swim, like a hallucination, through the kaleidoscope of repetitive human types, the face of Russian conscience, a face that I felt was the obverse of mine, imprinted with Russian lack of scruple. Once again I felt he must have seen me, but I didn't let on. "You ought to say hello," chorused my inner voice, my outer sense of dignity, my conscience that had emigrated from the Soviet Union with me, and my civic voice that had been stripped of citizenship. Our faces came bobbing closer, unacknowledged by each other thus far, unrecognized amidst the other foreign faces. In the press of bodies retreat was impossible.

My lips were opening, my larynx taut, my shoulder muscles tensed to reach my hand out to him, but when we were once again separated by those four duellists' paces in the crowd that had momentarily parted, I chickened out. I couldn't figure out what it was he was looking at. It seemed he was looking straight at me, yet past me, as if he were looking straight through me. I was struck once again by the impression that he was blind. We were advancing on each other in the midday sun as if we were in pitch darkness or playing a game of blind man's buff.

At the last moment I couldn't bear it. My legs diverted me down a narrow gap between buildings, a blind side-street squeezed between the flanks of restaurants and encumbered with garbage bins. My furtive dash ended with me slipping on a piece of rotten cabbage, or something of that sort. Trying to keep my balance, I put my hand out to the slimy walls, smeared myself with some filth oozing down from overhead and landed in a heap of garbage from an overturned bin. Still clutching the *IHT*, my hand skidded over stinking asphalt spread with a liberal coating of either sheep or cat shit. I swore, slung the paper in a bin, and went straight back to my hotel on the seafront, the Hotel Neptune.

I couldn't say precisely how many hours I lay in the bath in an attempt to lather away the memory of the embarrassing meeting and subsequent tumble in the mire. From time to time I took a swig of smoky Jameson's bought at the Heathrow duty free. My skin prickled with moisture. Either it was sweat provoked by the memory of my blunder or just drops of condensation running down from my forehead into my eyes. My eyes, in turn, were red either from whiskey and steam or from tears of remorse. I cursed my selfishness and misanthropy. How the hell had we landed up in the same Middle Eastern hole, a place where you were bound to run into each other at some point? Anywhere else—New York, Paris, or Jerusalem—I would immediately have given myself the job of guide, showed him where to go, what to see, and where to stay. I felt embarrassed at the thought that here he was, an old man, at a loose end somewhere he didn't know with an ageing wife, who could barely stay on her feet, and trying to decipher the menus in the restaurants. I had thrown them to the wolves. He had noticed me. Of course he had. Three encounters were quite enough. He'd seen I didn't want to see him, and so had pretended not to notice me. And no amount of rationalizing along the lines of being blind to familiar faces in exotic locations or of vision being selective depending on one's intentions and desires would alter the fact.

But for all my sense of guilt at what had happened, I knew I couldn't have acted otherwise. I hadn't dragged myself all the way from England to spend a week nattering endlessly in the émigré equivalent of a communal kitchen with the most boring neighbor possible. Suddenly this pleasant, quite comfortable, yet unpretentious resort struck me as being symbolic of the narrowness and hopelessness of émigré life. Not just émigré life. Why had I been obliged back in Moscow to reckon with, talk to, meet and part company with, and then meet again this stupid, droning demagogue? Why had the existence of a common political enemy compelled us Russians to pretend we were as good as related to one another?

I suddenly felt I hated Mikhail Sergeyevich Grets. Not because he belonged to a different generation or because I had no time for his ideas, but simply I couldn't stand, never had been able to stand the way he spat when he talked, his filthy nails, his sweaty bald patch and pot belly. Under different historical circumstances, in a different civilization, one glance would have told us we were mutually incompatible, and we would never meet again. In the Russian emigration, however, we spent nearly twenty years concealing straightforward personal dislike under a cloak of fundamental differences in ideological stance and of the power of the generation gap.

The sharp aroma of whiskey in the bathroom swept me back on swirling clouds of steam to London. It would be misty back there now, in the evenings especially, when every tree in the parks grew a halo and seemed even more independent and detached from the outside world on its patch of lawn. And a light in a distant window gleaming through the mist or the thread of a neon light altered perspective by its visible proximity, so heightening the feeling of space and at the same time of the hypnotic accessibility of objects on the horizon. I reached for the bottle. It was empty.

This was the point where I ought to have stopped, but I was drawn outside, back to England, as if the very waters of the Channel lapped outside my room in the Hotel Neptune. Outside, though, the little town was bathed in the warm Southern night. I moved unconsciously from bar to bar towards the center, towards that same small square where I had encountered Grets. I was drawn there the way a murderer is driven back to the scene of his crime by the urge to correct a poorly-constructed story. In the light of the lamps, overhead spotlights, and fat funereal candles on restaurant tables, the two-story complex of cafés and discos reminded me of the stalls, boxes, and balconies of a gigantic theater. The light on the faces made them look like theatrical masks. In an outburst of drunken sincerity and emotion, I wanted to tear the mask off this world that pretended to be so two-dimensional and simple in the daylight, but with the onset of darkness was transformed into a cunning shadow play. I, who in the hardness of my heart and out of revulsion, had virtually condemned my old acquaintance to death, now tried to make amends for my heartlessness by hurling imprecations at the mechanistic artificiality of our civilization, at our alienation in general. I wanted to tear away the iron mask of civilization and snuggle up to the warm, yielding body of nature.

Instead, I attached myself to the warm, yielding body of an American tourist. I met her in one of the bars after I had launched brazenly into a Russian rendition of an aria from either *The Flederwidow* or *The Merrymaus*, "to wear a mask is ever my fate." I heard an American drawl: "Jesus, this place is just crawling with Russians!" I was about to dispute the point, but had to admit that she was absolutely right—the place was crawling with them, and with Americans, too, for that matter. I told her she was right, and because the place was crawling with both Russians and Americans there was nothing for it but to drink Bloody Marys, made from Russian vodka and American tomato juice. She said that was her name, Mary. That was the last thing either of us said. We soon found the Bloody bit of the Mary to be superfluous and started drinking vodka neat without any bloody tomatoes or other such Americanisms. We rounded off this festival of international friendship in my hotel room, where we spent the night mixing juices of quite another sort with a special frenzy. This was communication beyond considerations of ideology and generation. Early next morning she had vanished without trace.

Actually, I'm wrong. Nothing disappears without trace, be it a stain on somebody else's sheets or on your own reputation. The sun, as I've said before, elides the distance between objects. Fate, like a cunning storyteller, brings together in the one dénouement utterly disparate events and circumstances. And this has to be paid for by a loss of opportunities, the way sunburn is the price of a tan.

After our fatal encounter on the African coast, I realized I could never accept an invitation from the Grets household to go and write at their villa in Greece. They had inherited it from Mrs. Grets's family, the Popandopouloses. Sofya Konstantinovna was, as I think I've mentioned, the daughter of a Greek millionaire from Theodosia. He spent half his life in Russia, was a connoisseur of Russian literature and art, dabbled as a collector and knew Diaghilev and Benois. He had left a modest bequest—enough to set up a bursary—to help needy Russian émigré intellectuals. It was sufficient to pay travel expenses and full board, from one to three months, in a luxurious house with marble columns (modeled on the Parthenon, of course) on Crete.

Cretin that I was, after being awarded that year's bursary,

I felt I had to turn it down. I couldn't bring myself to look at Grets's face oozing faith in humankind every morning at the breakfast table. Nor could I bear the memory of him looking lost as he stared at me with unseeing eyes under the African sun. My amorality did not allow for inconsistency when it came to questions of moral principle.

This was why when an envelope was delivered to my London address containing an official invitation and requesting a formal reply, there was nothing for it but to compose a lengthy refusal, in which after thanking the Popandopoulos Fund effusively for the honor it had bestowed upon me I explained that on this occasion I simply could not avail myself of Mr. and Mrs. Grets's hospitality. I had signed a contract with French radio that required my presence in Paris. (I had, indeed, signed a contract for a radio adaptation of my novel, but my presence in Paris was the last thing that was wanted.)

At the end of the letter I expressed the hope that I would be able to take up their generous offer at a future date and that we would meet in the not-too-distant future. Yours very etc., etc.

A few days later I received a reply by express mail from Mikhail Sergeyevich Grets. The text follows without further commentary.

> *Mea culpa,* Zinovy, *mea maxima culpa.* I antici-
> pated you would refuse, hoped that this cup of shame
> might pass from me. But no! I am an old fool and I
> have to confess that I have received my just deserts,
> *mea culpa!*
>
> My dear boy, the look of silent reproach in your
> eyes as you sat at your table, and when you were in
> the crowd and up on that gallery, will stay with me
> the rest of my life. Like a fool, I pretended not to see

you, the very person with whom I have always enjoyed exchanging a few words, swapping views (*sic!*) on current events. And I besmirched myself not once, but thrice; thrice pretended that I did not know you, denied you thrice on that damned pocket-handkerchief of a square.

How many times, dear boy, have I taken up my pen to apologize for my monstrously childish behavior, hoped, old fool that I am, to bump into you at one of our émigré talk-ins. I would explain myself at some conference or other. I thought I could smooth this silly episode over. All the time I was hoping against hope that I'd got away with it, that you hadn't seen me, and that if you had, you hadn't recognized me. One can do that, you know—see without noticing.

But when we received your courteous refusal to take up the Popandopoulos bursary, I knew the game was up. It was you, dear boy, gentleman that you are, who made me realize how deeply wounding my loutish behavior was. But it's so unnecessary. I know I'm a boor and utterly stiff-necked and that my behavior was unforgivable, but I do assure you, dear boy, that Sofya and I love you dearly and hold you in the highest regard.

I apologize abjectly and unreservedly. *Mea culpa!* My apologies—*ad absurdum.* It was my mendacity, depravity, and the insatiability of my lusts. Would you believe me if I told you I was being unfaithful to my devoted companion, my fellow warrior on the ideological front, and medical orderly in the trenches of the emigration, in short—to my wife, Sofya Konstantinovna? I love Sofie with all my soul, mind, and civic conscience. But my heart, dear boy, began a desperate race with my greying hair. And the devil beneath my ribs drove me to that African resort where our paths so unfortunately chanced to cross.

The American girl you undoubtedly noticed at my side during our fateful encounter was the cause of my unforgivable snub. I funked it. With your excellent English, you were bound to engage her in small talk and, quite unconsciously, let slip that I was married and that would mark the ignominious end to my brief affair. I met her at a human rights conference.

She fell in love with me for what I'd been through, and I embroidered the more lurid details. Humiliating as it is, dear boy, to have to go into all this, but the fact of the matter is I was scared stiff. If you had started talking, that would have been the end of my legend. And so, dear boy, I started that silly schoolboy game. As soon as I saw you at the table I began putting a telescope to a blind eye and behaving as though you weren't there. Shameful, utterly, utterly shameful!

Except that it was a complete mental aberration; I cannot explain this sexual escapade at my age. Should you still harbor any grudging sentiments towards me, my dear, perhaps I can put them to rest with the information that nothing in this life goes unpunished. After the incident with you, the young American lady and I quarreled violently. She insisted she only wanted a *café frappé,* while at my age I need three square meals a day. She slammed the door on me and vanished without even saying goodbye. Probably she was picked up by some young yahoo. Not even probably. I know for certain she was, because I managed to find the hotel where she spent that night (the Neptune,

down on the seafront, you may remember it) and the
porter told me she didn't spend the night alone. Slut!
Still, *mea culpa.*
    Ever yours,
    Mikh. Serg. Grets."

1987

Translated by Frank Williams

HOOKS

IN AMERICA I WOULD NEVER RUN ACROSS PEOPLE LIKE HIM; they fly in circles too lofty for me to reach. And the Soviets are still reluctant to let such a person visit Tel Aviv. As an émigré, I'd only encounter them in Europe, here in London or in Paris.

But somehow I can never get used to them—it is either their casual familiarity, as if nothing untoward had occurred, or the reverse, the long, tragic face, as if you were attending your own funeral. That Moscow was, for me, irrecoverable was never discussed, as if the two of us just happened to be in London for a while and, whereas he had to get back shortly, certain urgent business compelled me to stay on. At least he didn't launch into the predictable discourse on the destiny of the West as seen through Russian eyes, the standard counterblast to émigré ideas on the destiny of Russia as seen through Western eyes. His own eyes were semi-transparent, dangerous-feeling, as though if you peered deeply into them myopia would set in and you'd never find your way out.

But he kept those eyes averted; he wasn't at ease either. He didn't know how to behave with me. I flattered myself that he might be feeling some shame in my presence. But perhaps I was merely assigning him noble feelings to put myself in a good light. Or it may have been an effect of the difference in our status: he was, after all, an industrial expert on an official exchange visit, the holder of a great State Prize, the honored representative of Soviet history, whereas I, a wandering émigré, had been consigned by that same state to the blacklist with the dubious label of "rootless cosmopolite". Even that term belonged to his vocabulary, not mine—the vocabulary of the old wartime Stalinist generation. But, like most exiles, I was given to striking up acquaintance with strangers, and in hopes of being understood and accepted I would slavishly accommodate myself to their speech.

For someone like me, our meeting had the air of an ideological duel; he on the other hand, must have found my agitation fascinating. He would keep his eyes averted; then suddenly, seemingly offhand, he would touch my shoulder lightly, or nudge my elbow, till I began to think that I had been wide of the mark in imagining any kind of official arrogance in his actions, or calculated condescension in his conversation.

Not that there was any real conversation. Actually, I couldn't understand why we were meeting at all. He had introduced himself as the uncle of my wife's high-school sweetheart back in Moscow. To that I found little to say; I thought of Yesenin's line: "I am your nephew, you are all my uncles," and Eichenvald's: "All men are brothers; me, I'm a cousin." But poetry was not one of his interests. On the other hand, he wasn't taking the occasion to make the usual Soviet visitor's request for either of the naked truths that Moscow banned: Solzhenitsyn's books or Soho's porn displays.

We were sitting in his seedy hotel room looking at one another with the simulated amicability of the dentist's waiting room. I couldn't make out why he said nothing—was it fear, plain indifference, or some inherent inability to start up a conversation? I repeated to myself my wife's admonitions on similar occasions: don't worry about him, he's been in this situation before; he'll tell you what he wants soon enough. He was clearly not at all discomfited by the protracted pause, and like anyone accustomed to an iron curtain of silence he transferred to his companion the sense of guilt for the break in communication. It is in the nature of words to abhor silence; forgetting my wife's injunctions, I filled the air with overexcited and largely inconsequential talk.

"What really amazes me is my indifference. Actually, when I do feel drawn to Moscow it's the earlier Moscow I picture. What goes on there now, in fact, doesn't really interest me much. I mean, even the old notion that it's the people who stayed behind who betrayed us, and we émigrés are the heroes carrying on the battle without them—even that seductive old idea has lost its savor; those who betrayed us are no longer crucial to our happiness. If we get homesick, it's not for our actual home but the home of memory."

"As to life in Moscow," he finally resolved to interrupt my rambling meditations, "I would quote from a poem I prize highly, by Mezhirov: 'The acts we put on may be sham, but you have to remember we're working without a safety net—one false step and we're smashed to smithereens.'"

I was silent. Well, of course. To hear them talk, their only concern is Absolute Truth, unlike the materialistic West, with its relativism and hypocrisy; prophetic fire, the endless task, all that. They might lie to each other, but it's always about great matters, for noble purposes; perhaps superficially, to the outsider's eye, things don't look right, but deep down inside it's all real and true. "Smashed to smithereens"—the danger justifying the ends and the means. Yes, indeed. I just hoped he wasn't going to start discoursing about "inner freedom". It seemed it was business as usual back there.

"The day they acknowledge what they did in the Hitler-Stalin Pact, that's the day I'll . . ." I began, but I dried up. I recognized that look. My father, a communist and a Jew, who lost a leg in the war, used to look at me that way when, in the heat of argument, I would blurt that if Hitler hadn't stirred up Russian patriotism, Stalin and the whole Soviet system would have gone into the dustbin of history long ago. I wasn't afraid of my father's belt, much less his raised voice, but his tears made me feel terrible. It was with those same eyes, those pink-tinged lids, that the Muscovite visitor looked at me now. That was the worst thing, that defenseless look of a person who suddenly realizes he is being viewed critically. I shouldn't have mentioned the war. That glance had betrayed a bitter nostalgia for those days. For him, the war must have been a unique period of freedom, when fate had granted his spirit the gift of a genuine patriotism; when it had been possible to defend the fatherland without orders from above or a pistol in the back of the neck: when he was issued a gun of his own and bullets to strike down what were enemies of the people in the true sense of the term, not in Stalin's. He might have been my own father—and I had absolutely nothing to say to him.

"Could you possibly help me find a certain little thing I want in London?" he asked in a pleading tone, and I sighed with relief. So—he, too, was after some piece of scarce merchandise; he was no exception after all. It just might have been conceivable that a man who'd worked his way up to responsible posts, titles, and decorations could remain a decent human even over there—well, it's nice to have one's skepticism validated, I said to myself. The old motherland can always come through with a fresh example of Darwinian principle—the evolution of the worthy idealistic Bolshevik model into an ape of material greed in response to his environment. Determinism shaping subspecies *homo sovieticus*—an animal with a highly spiritual ideological mask over a primitive avaricious grimace. Yes, squirm as you like, you grow the way conditions ordain. It's pitiable, I suppose. But somehow my own spirit wasn't up to purging its revulsion.

"You couldn't take me to Oxford Street, could you?" asked the Soviet gent when I, despite my interior harangue, spoke aloud of my readiness to help.

"What part of Oxford Street?"

"Where the shops are."

"It's all shops."

"Fine, let's go there, then." He added in a confidential whisper, "I want some hooks."

"Hooks? What sort of hooks?" I asked, somewhat flabbergasted.

"Fishing hooks," he explained imperturbably and, rising slightly from his chair, poked two fingers into an inconspicuous watch pocket in his trousers; there was something tucked away in there, deep down, that refused to be brought to light. At last he withdrew a cellophane packet about the size of a matchbox. It, in turn, contained a piece of paper torn from a school exercise book and folded into four. I followed all these operations as if watching a conjurer at work. He proffered the folded note. On it enigmatic English words and names had been written with calligraphic exactitude; to the left of these was a no less puzzling column of figures with hieroglyphic curlicues—or were they drawings? It all looked like some spy cipher to me, and only served to intensify the false atmosphere of intimacy between us. Could he possibly have been sent by Moscow to recruit me into the K.G.B.'s Russian Literature Service, as we called it—to ask me to add my reports on London émigré activity to the files stacked inside the world's biggest humanities collection, the Lubyanka security headquarters? I looked up in alarm.

"It's a list. English fishing hooks with sizes. Can you give me a hand?" He moved his finger about the paper. Once again I began to flounder in that translucent gaze, trying to swim out of turbid water, keeping clear of whirlpools and shoals. They'd obviously gone off their heads over there, perched with their elite salaries beside the well-stocked ponds at their Politburo country dachas. Couldn't they manage with Soviet hooks? They must figure that even the cunning old pike of Russian folklore could never resist an elegant, unbreakable English hook. Maybe they heard of them in the handbook by Aksakov, our nineteenth-century Compleat Angler; for all his

Slavophile outlook, he may have gone Anglophile himself when it came to recommending fishhooks.

"I can't go back to Moscow without hooks," whimpered this man, this apparent adult. There it was again: Soviet civilization turns everybody into a child where *things* are concerned; *things* are the toys of civilization, and the citizen of a vast country that hasn't many of them acts like a deprived child. You feel sorry for him, and irritated, and you know you can't shake him off. Ridiculing their puritanism as sham, though, is like calling a hungry man a hypocrite for taking a job advertising meat on a sandwich board. Like children everywhere, they simply must have material proof of their own idealism: thus Soviet people are materialistic idealists. Children have to be indulged, life won't give them a chance like this again—so we strode out in search of English fishhooks.

London was deluged in one of those spinning storms of rain and light you find only on this island, where the wind blows from four directions at once and you never know which way to turn to shield your eyes from the blinding droplets. We hung, as it were, in the timelessness of streaming rain, detached from the earth, pressed against one another, heads bent together like a pair of lovers: he'd left his umbrella in the hotel. We couldn't be bothered to go back for it, so the hurricane of rain and wind bore us along the side streets under one umbrella. The closer we became welded by the weather, the more alien I sensed his body to be, pressed against my shoulder in his smelly gabardine mackintosh and the sort of tartan cap that unversed tourists take to be typically English. He grated on me because of the absence of physical distance between us; I couldn't get free of him. To do that I would have to snag him with those special hooks, and we simply could not find any. These hooks turned out to be most rare and intricate, and the salesmen startlingly ignorant and rude. As we trudged for mile after mile along shopping streets, I subsided into a despairing resentment. I shook feverishly, either because of the penetrating wind or because of the intense exasperation I felt at the whole enterprise I'd been dragged into by that old business between my wife and the nephew of this Soviet fisherman.

One umbrella was clearly inadequate: my companion was wearing a decent raincoat at least, whereas I had casually donned a corduroy jacket, which, as it absorbed the moisture, grew heavier and heavier, like an old soak under the Charing Cross arches. My back ached, my shoes squished, my throat was raw, and I cursed the Soviet regime for its false liberalism in letting perverts with English-fishhook fetishes loose on London. We advanced in rushes, dashing through one glassy curtain of rain only to run into another, and as we halted to catch our breath in this jerky course we seemed to be on different landings of the same flight of stairs. No, it was as if two glass-cabined elevators had stopped for a second in a dark shaft and we gazed at one another through their walls: was it even conceivable we both lived under the same roof? Bound together, kin forever? That was all I needed of hell.

"Don't worry, I'm not trying to persuade you to go back," said my Soviet gent. He didn't mean to the Old Country, he meant to Oxford Street, which we had left farther and farther behind—a mistake, in his view, since all shops that could possibly exist must be there. I could have no objection: I really didn't know where to go next. I'd got well off my planned route.

"I know what this rain reminds me of," he said, wiping his face with a handkerchief as we were waiting out the next squall under an arch at Piccadilly Circus. "This London rain reminds me of mosquito netting and the evening mist after a hot day at the dacha. It's just come back to me: your wife used to visit my nephew at the dacha. That was where I first saw her, maybe the last time, too. A slim schoolgirl she was, like a dandelion. They were walking together arm in arm, towards the terrace. Through a sort of haze like this rain. I was sitting with my sister on the terrace. Mist all round, you know, makes distances hard to judge. Mosquitoes and moths were flying around the lamp, and there was a sweet smell of paraffin. I remember that so well."

He stopped as if hoping for an answering burst of lyricism. As it was, this nephew, whoever he might be, was getting on my nerves. "Poor boy," my companion would say whenever he mentioned my wife's adolescent admirer. I resolved to curtail these nostalgic evocations of dacha life at least.

"After three emigrations, from one country to another," I said, "my yearning for the Old Country long ago lost any geographical dimension. It's not connected physically with any one point on the earth's surface. My normal state of mind, generally speaking, is rather like the indisposition of middle age: it's a kind of equilibrium, when one agonizing pain is balanced by another, newer one, which we know perfectly well we'll ignore as a third one looms up."

"But where on earth is Eros?" he broke in, as if rebuking me for excessive intellectualism in my reflections. He was pointing, however, at the wooden hoarding in the center of the square. Black Eros—the winged messenger with his arrow of love, balanced on one foot on the top of the fountain in the center of Piccadilly Circus, that symbol of gay old London— was gone from behind the planking. I had to explain that Eros had been sent off for restoration. Eros was under repair, the fountain of the soul was dry, only intellect sparkled in neon signs through the shrouding rain. Britannia was poor and stingy; everyone was on his own.

"Won't I see Eros at all this time, then?" He shook a mournful head. Like all Soviet tourists, he further annoyed me with his rustic raptures over cliché London—the red buses, the black taxis, the bobbies in their crested helmets. I felt an imbecile urgency to maintain the reputation of my émigré life in those alien Russian eyes, as if to say: "We have everything here, there's nothing you can't get. Especially rare and intricate fishhooks." With a heavy sigh, I darted into the swirling rain.

It enveloped us in a dense, wavering veil, solidly separating off the rest of the world, which might have been anywhere: England, Russia, ancient Rome. I calculated that we were on Pall Mall, where the Jules Verne novel starts—what was it, *Twenty Thousand Days Under the Sea* or *Eighty Thousand Leagues Around the World?* The snowy-white columns of the club buildings gleamed through the bathysphere of rain as they loomed over us like Arctic icebergs, mist-enshrouded, and, as Captain Nemo might have done, I wanted to cry, "To hell with this mercantile civilization!" Retreating from the elements, we found ourselves in an arcade, where the window of another tackle shop floated before our eyes like the porthole of an aquarium. The salesman luring us inside could have been Captain Nemo himself, or a Russian bog monster. He seemed to be expecting us. He put on his tortoise-shell glasses and spent a long time chewing his lip over our crumpled list of magic figures and markings. Finally he informed us, with the solemnity of an oracle, that he did have these hooks but that "they bend the other way."

"That doesn't matter," I hastened to explain this enigmatic phrase to my companion. "It's like driving on the left— it's all relative. From the Russian viewpoint, they bend the way you want, you see what I mean?" By way of visual illustration, I absurdly twisted my head around nearly backward. I just wanted to make clear that the problem was resolved and I would go no farther. In the little shop it was dry, rather dark, and deserted as we sat down to wait at a table in the corner.

There was something in that interior reminiscent of the Ark, pitching under the lashing assault of the storm. Around us were gleaming glass cases of mounted fish; nets and harpoons hung in the corners, fishing poles sprouted everywhere like exotic bamboo, and, most important, gigantic showcases held hooks of all sizes, shapes, and tints overlapping like metallic scales. My companion in his sodden raincoat reminded me of a shivering *dachnik*, stranded on a suburban station platform after missing the electric train.

And I remembered where I'd seen exactly the same suffering expression, reproach mixed with hope. Those same grimaces had been displayed by the old repairman in the typewriter shop on Kuznetsky Most, when I brought my Olympia to him for the last time before I left the country. The very same heavy rain, Muscovite variety, had beset his premises, too, replete as it was with objects no less exotic than those in this tackle shop. How he'd fussed about, sighing and shaking his head, when he found out what far lands I was quitting Moscow for. How he'd started unscrewing the casing with excessive roughness to conceal his trembling fingers as they tugged out the accumulated dirt, hair, and assorted rubbish.

"You've got a cat at home, then," he'd grumbled. "I can tell what any household is like by the stuff in the typewriter."

We had no cats at home—it was me going bald, not a cat—but never mind; he was just filling up a tense silence with his mutterings. Then he got out a jug of alcohol, but instead of using it to clean the keys he ran some tap water into it and banged down two glasses. I remember the light, acrid smell of the spirits and the mustiness of the basement shop, his tear-filled eyes and the network of blood vessels on his flaccid, alcoholic cheeks. And the dim gleam of the part in his brilliantined hair. An hour later, his hair sticking up wildly by now, he was recounting for the umpteenth time his exploits as an air ace.

But finally he couldn't hold back, he burst the net of restraint: he had, he said, a Tatar friend—the carriage on the man's typewriter even went backwards, the Muslim way—but he had no plans to leave, even though Stalin had moved him to Siberia for a while. What was wrong with me, couldn't I sit still? He and the Tatar used to go fishing at a reservoir a mere hundred kilometers from Moscow, and he'd feel homesick even there; on the way back, the very mention of Moscow made his heart beat faster. How could anybody leave—forever? He just couldn't see that. He'd be glad to take me to that reservoir with a net, to get some big fish. Or in winter maybe, to sit out all night with a line through the ice. He'd found *yeriki* there, spots where the ice seals off the water and all the fish are caught inside as in a bucket: you could take them out with your bare hands.

I remember his oddly intent stare—and mine, shifty, though it should have been the other way round. I remember us sitting there for a long time, like now: close kin and at the same time totally alien. I couldn't argue with him, because the only ideas he could comprehend were foreign to me, and I can't convey alien thoughts in my own words.

The exotic word *yeriki* had taken me aback considerably—was it the resonance with "eureka"? I even took the trouble to consult Dal's dictionary. I felt like that old gudgeon (or whatever inhabits Moscow reservoirs), gasping under the ice in those *yeriki*. Meanwhile outside, the yellow houses on Kuznetsky Most were wet with rain. Yellow houses—Moscow isn't a fairy-tale snow-white city, it's a city of yellow houses. It was grim hauling my typewriter home past those sodden yellow façades; what sort of person was it who could construe your longing for peace of mind and for freedom as treachery? I remembered my fear, not of treason, or prison, but of becoming one of them myself, the fear of being defined, my fate ordained, by others.

But how I longed to be back under the lowering Moscow skies at this moment; for any fear contains the hope of release from that fear, and the memory of that feeling of hope, which accompanied all the years I spent there, overcame the memory of fear. That insistent sense of a hope lost forever is in itself punishment for my decision to free myself permanently from fear. And lost along with that hope was the avidity of eye and finger, the pleasure, with which this stranger from my Soviet past was now picking over the shining fishhooks on the table. It was for the sake of this scene then—to witness another's appetite for my new life when I myself had grown blasé—that I had dragged along with this venerable Soviet official under an English cloudburst. It was for the joy of recognition in the eyes of the other—a perverse sense of nearness, no matter whether with friend or enemy. (No one is closer to being a sworn enemy than your best friend; the two can be almost the same.)

"You've saved a man's life, you should know," said the Soviet fellow, looking up at me as if guessing my thoughts about him. "You've saved a human being. Thank you."

"No need to exaggerate," I managed to bring out with affected nonchalance. "You'd have survived somehow without English hooks."

"Me? I would, of course. But what about my nephew? Poor boy." And his chin began to quiver. He reached for his handkerchief. The shopkeeper, off behind his counter, gazed through his tortoise-shell glasses at the vast window spattered with raindrops, pretending not to notice our corner mutterings in some incomprehensible and unreal tongue: for me, this heightened the sense of conspiracy, of the confessional, that surrounded the words of this elderly man, who had suddenly lost all traits of the Soviet. All that remained was his bewilderment at the perversity of fate and a mute plea for sympathy, nothing more.

The mention of the nephew, again, annoyed me so much that at first I didn't take in what he was saying—about cards and billiards, about Dostoyevsky's *Gambler*, a woman, and underworld Moscow, and the odd idea of escaping from a politicized world into some sort of casino where stakes were high and payment was not in cash but in kind—and what an effort it had taken to get that list of English fishhooks out of prison. In jail they keep accounts their own way, he was saying: you don't pay up, your throat gets slit.

At length it began to dawn on me what my former countryman was talking about: these double-damned hooks were not destined for privileged bureaucrats to go catch sturgeon in Kremlin ponds, no. Lord knows *who* would be fishing with them, in what troubled waters. These hooks were the equivalent of beads for savages; they were treasury notes, legal tender, hard currency in the jailhouse banking system of incorrigible gamblers. The nephew was such a gambler, and he was in jail. "If I hadn't looked you up in London, the poor boy . . ." and he made a gesture near his throat.

"You know," he went on, "I'd have washed my hands of that boy long since; he's a hopeless case." My companion snorted into his handkerchief. "But not long before he was arrested he took me to one of those awful restaurants I can't stand—people stuffing themselves, champing, belching, the orchestra hammering out some execrable stuff . . . I looked around at it all, and I quoted a line from, I think it's Heinrich Heine: 'To think the Redeemer died on the cross for these swine—what a waste!' My nephew smiled a little, and said, 'No, my dear uncle, your Heine was wrong. Decent folk can take care of their own salvation; it was precisely to save such miserable worms as these that the Fisherman got himself on the hook.' Imagine! And I'd figured that good-for-nothing for a fool. How wrong can a man be?"

He began stowing the English fishhooks about his person.

1987

Translated by Alan Myers

CRICKET

I

"To understand cricket, dear boy, you have to dismiss the idea that you score by hitting the wicket. Because in cricket you score by making runs. What counts is how often you can run from one end of the pitch to the other while your opponents try and hit the wicket you are running towards. D'you see?" No, I didn't. I still hadn't understood the slightest thing about the game, though I had grasped the elegance of its absurd logic: its zaniness stemmed from its simplicity. It would be easier to understand if it was more complicated. Nothing is simpler to accept than alien complexities, if only because we tend to respect the word of a stranger. The further and wider you hit the ball, the more room there is for maneuver. The defender scores, not the attacker. Clear?

The bowler ran up and bowled at the batsman, who looked gigantic against the absurdly small wicket he was defending. I could work out a mass of details, but had only a fuzzy notion of how they added up. It was like repeating for the hundredth time the same laughably simple phrase in a foreign language, when you understand its component parts but cannot knit words together into the slippery unpredictability of syntax. In a daze I stared at the pitch, its grass as green as envy, the sky a bright blue, and the cricketers clad in ridiculously virginal whites. The movements of the players crisscrossing the green were equally eerie. The fact that the ball was scarcely visible during play made it seem as though the two teams were locked in some mysterious conspiracy, a strange collective rite that formed no perceptible whole and had no visible rhyme or reason. They might have been trying to catch the Invisible Man, for all I could tell.

My guide to the art of cricket was sixty-year-old Arthur Simons, a sub-editor on the weekly paper *The Browser*. He gazed at me through ironical blue eyes, in which summer-colored skies mingled with clouds. The more Pimm's he drank, the more his eyes misted over, the clouds thickening as time went on. To explain Pimm's to an outsider is as hard as to tell what cricket is all about. Theoretically, it is a kind of English Campari. But whereas Campari is a scarlet bitter that can be drunk with soda or cut with orange juice, Pimm's is on the sweetish side and the murky color of stewed fruit. That's the idea: stewed fruit, which the English stuff with the first thing that comes into their head: lemon or cucumber. Why not cucumber, after all? I'm not sure but I think that true Pimm's aficionados even drink it with radishes. At all events, it ends up resembling *okroshka,* that cold Russian vegetable soup based on bread beer, and having nothing in common with Italian Campari.

Anyhow, all these explanations of mine, like any unsuccessful version of an untranslatable detail of life peculiar to England, create the wrong impression of that sunny day in June. Arthur and I were lounging in white deck chairs at an English cricket match. Those eyes of his were so blue that a cricket ball batted into the sky could lose itself in them. But they also revealed that he had nowhere left to retreat, no way out, no room for maneuver. He was a hay-fever sufferer: he wheezed and sniffled constantly, and he buried himself in his handkerchief after every gulp from his glass. He was in the kind of state where any bystander would take him as being on the verge of death: that asthmatic rasp, those reddened eyelids, the end of his tongue forever busy in a snakelike licking of the lips: it lent him the air of something soon to be beyond the grave, cast out from this world of ours.

I, by comparison, a Soviet emigré with my fig leaf of a British passport, still looked bearable, almost a habitué of this cricket club. I felt moreover as if I was attending the first night of my own show, since I had appeared in the last issue of his weekly as an author, "his author", to boot. For I was Arthur Simons's very own literary find, though actually he had dug me out from the *Times Literary Supplement,* which had long been using me for roughly the same purpose, whenever things exotic and foreign appeared on the London scene, some cultural freak suitable for a fairground booth (such as an Israeli production of Otto Weininger, the Viennese anti-Semitic Jew and misogynist suicide, whose work *Sex and Character* was based on the notion that Judaism represents the feminine principle in mankind). At such times, with my Russian past and dual British-Israeli citizenship, I would be dusted down and brought out to write a review.

Here I was being treated as a prima donna with an exotic sophistication that could only be compared to my own literary enterprises. To be invited to their annual cricket match, between the editorial team and their publishers, was an honor in its own right; it was attended by all the literati of publishing London, and everyone was willing to smirk graciously at my sallies in the style of Weininger on the subject of Russia, also a feminine object: Russia in its present false pregnancy with freedom, its premenstrual tension resulting from the inevitable emigration of Jews, and its inevitable literary climax. The more time passed the more I felt at home, a fully paid-up member of the cricket team, as it were, nodding my head knowingly whenever Arthur bent intimately in my direction, wittily pointing out that "our" batsman was now Harold Pinter who, with his genius for the silence in dialogue, would demonstrate that pauses were the key to an understanding of cricket.

"From the spectator's viewpoint," continued Arthur, not lifting his tearstained gaze from the cricket pitch, "it seems a game of elusive lightness and grace. But when you are out there facing the bowler, your knees shake. The cricket ball is a terrifying weapon. It is small but heavy and hard to the touch. It whistles through the air like a cannonball. You feel you are about to have your brains blown out before the eyes of the public. Everyone appears to be waiting for you to be crippled. And there's nothing you can do. It's a terrible feeling, dear boy, terrible." I saw him grip the sides of his deck chair with his jaundiced hands. One of the reasons I liked Arthur Simons was that he was one of the few Englishmen who did not have that condescending way of pretending to lower himself to the level of the Russian barbarian that is normally displayed by British intellectuals, who will heap scorn on their own country merely to carry on talking to the curious but unlettered alien in their midst. So when Arthur spoke of the aggressiveness of the English hidden by a mask of aloof kindliness I believed him. He addressed me as if talking to himself rather than me, as if I was his equal in the circle of the elect. But just then Joan made her entry, at the other end of the green.

I had never expected her to turn up here. Or rather, she obviously did not expect to find me at the cricket match and her surprise at seeing me seemed to tell me just how out of place I was. That was the effect she had been having on me ever since our first meeting. She had been my first true Londoner in the sense that she had entrée into those circles where people like me are not to be found, a Russian Jew arrived in London from Moscow by way of Jerusalem. To paraphrase Groucho Marx, I could not help feeling a secret admiration for places where I was not accepted: it meant there was something worthwhile about them, if only the fact that I was not accepted. In short, the grass is always greener. . . .

My meeting with Joan had coincided with the period in my London life when I imagined that I already belonged, that I was no longer the outsider, the kid from down the street pressing his nose against someone else's window where a party is going on. The foreigner is always looking in from the outside, squashing his nose against the pane: always the alien monster. I had kidded myself that I had broken away from my Russian past even if I had not yet found the words to describe my soul's new state of being. I felt that at least I had stopped translating my new life into my old language, I was no longer simply aping the English way of doing things. I seemed to be thinking in English while continuing to speak Russian. But isn't this an illusion, this separation of thought and word? Can one really speak an "English" kind of Russian? Don't all English turns of phrase evaporate like invisible ink as soon as you stop speaking English? Can you translate into your own language things that obsess and bewitch you simply because they are untranslatable? Can what is not yours become your own? How can you take in something that is alien, if what is alien is by definition that which cannot be absorbed?

Joan proceeded along the opposite side of the green, identifiable a mile away by the demonstratively ill-assorted clothes she wore. Her umbrella was perhaps the only detail borrowed from the conventional wardrobe of a lady at a cricket match. The umbrella was black, an ordinary umbrella, probably quite elegant in itself, with an ivory handle, all silk and sophistication, but designed for the rain and, most importantly, black. For that matter she was dressed entirely in black, the done thing at that time among her crowd, the narrow circle of those who considered people who were not of their number as being not true Londoners. Her black skirt trailed across the grass like a ballroom dress but her black jacket was cut like a man's, with padded shoulders and hanging open. She was an unforgettable sight, with her bowler hat and the red forelock peering out from under it, an eccentric. As always, she dressed so much the way that is not done that you might be forgiven for thinking that it was the done thing to do so. At that moment, I had no doubt she was the very epitome of English taste and refinement.

Recalling the provocative eccentricity that she paraded across the cricket field in her preposterous gear, doubt creeps over me: in the eyes of the other spectators she must have seemed a bit flaky, slightly missing the point. Perhaps what I took for eccentric chic was just the get-up of someone who was mildly touched: it was as if she had found her wardrobe at a dump. In blatant disorder she had shoved on old lace together with jeans, a dinner jacket and T-shirt, a cabaret bowler hat and the high laced boots of a Victorian schoolgirl. On the snowy backdrop of cricketing whites her black rig made her look like a housefly on a bedsheet. She made her way towards us where we sat in our deck chairs, not along the edge of the green but striding brazenly across the corner of the cricket pitch; and I felt the rising irritation of players and spectators alike. If she wasn't careful she might be attacked by a player as he fielded the ball or the ball might half-accidentally strike her on her hat or some other sensitive spot. Play practically stopped. Here too she succeeded in gaining the limelight.

I rose from my deck chair and waved her a greeting. Heads swung round in my direction and stared. Even from my position at the far end of the pitch from her, I could see how her face changed. Her gaze, which a moment before had been wandering somewhere around the horizon, totally indifferent to the stares of the spectators, stopped in its tracks. Her eyes widened, starting out of their sockets as if trying to escape beyond the gates to the cricket ground. But it was too late: we were already being stared at. "Zinik, darling, what brings you here? I would never have expected!"

Of course she wouldn't have expected. Earlier that morning I had tried to persuade her to come to a cricket match but in her half-sleep she had not even been interested enough to ask who was playing whom. She had muttered something about an important business commitment during the day and that in any case sport was not something she was really interested in. It was sort of, she had mumbled, and anyway she wasn't really, you know . . . It had sounded hollow, given her acute and demonstrative Anglophilia. She couldn't imagine that it was this cricket match I was coming to, which in any case was not so much a cricket match as a society occasion, where people like myself would not be found. Or so she must have thought.

From the moment we met, Joan treated me as a confidant of exotic origin. I was her very own Russian, for personal and exclusive use, at any time of the night or day. "My Russian," she would say, referring to me at social gatherings. "My Russian, you know, my Russian Zinik from Moscow." As if I was her tame bear imported from Siberia, her poodle from the Moscow English Club. As if I had never been a Londoner. We all need an exotic past, if only to lend a touch of the unique to our drab present. We all need others to see us from the outside, and that was my role so far as she was concerned. Apart from all my other virtues, my Russian origins guaranteed her the inviolability of the confessional, whatever secrets she might blurt out to me; it was obvious that the emigré circles in which my gossip traveled did not intersect with the London society she moved in. She kept me locked up in the boudoir of her confessions. But now the door to it had opened and we had both emerged into the gaze of the cricketing public, with our trousers down, as it were—although, admittedly, both in different poses.

My growing friendship with Joan had coincided with my break-up with Silvia. It was in fact Silvia who had brought us together, by inviting Joan to her New Year's party. The previous summer Joan had rented a house from a Mrs. MacLearmont in Argyllshire and naturally enough the latter had run on to her about an extravagant Russian relative. Silvia was only a very distant relative, but with the help of a large amount of whisky the Scottish aunt had long ago been lured into believing in the indissoluble bonds between the Clan MacLearmont and the Russian Lermontovs (their ancestors having been Scottish Catholics who had fled to Russia). As a result Silvia had managed to secure a British passport. Since in our day and age all real people must number at least one Russian in their circle of friends, as soon as Joan returned to London she phoned Silvia with greetings from the aunt, and invited herself over. The two immediately declared themselves soul sisters, yet after the New Year's Eve party they had never met again. London is apt to make soul mates draw apart, it is a place where everyone seeks their opposite.

That evening Silvia was all over a half-forgotten former dissident from her Moscow years and man of the historical moment, as if he had been her best friend—the collapse of the Soviet Empire had flooded London with former dissenters who had done time in Soviet prison camps and mental hospitals. No sooner had the Iron Curtain slightly lifted its hem than Silvia herself began hopping over to Moscow on her British passport. Whenever she returned to London, she would sweep in with the most unlikely chaff of the latest revolutionary intelligentsia. With her feverish flights to Moscow, her frantic clinging to every Soviet who crossed her path in London, and the general stir she created, she looked like a castaway on a foreign shore, thirsting indiscriminately for company. For my part I had become a voluntary hermit, consciously and deliberately going native in the jungle of the diaspora, embracing every manifestation of local color. Thus I ceased to exist for her, though I was her only really close acquaintance. She was trying to melt into the majority of revolutionary Russians who had been on the run from the Soviet authorities, whereas I was trying to join a select minority by exacerbating my British insularity through the tight little circle of snobs from the privileged classes, like Joan.

At that New Year's party I had been sitting on the carpet between her and Joan, whom I can remember telling, when she asked why I did not visit Moscow again, "It would be like going back to your divorced wife." All the time I was following Silvia with my eyes as she moved in across the cushions on her visiting Moscow dissident. I recall the wandering smile on her lips—the smile of a victor, like someone at school who hides from her classmates the answer to an arithmetic problem: those shining and predatory eyes, confident that her victim is in her claws, and that resonant aggressive note in her voice, warning you she might go for your throat. How quickly she and that idiot from Moscow had got it together. There they were together: the only real Muscovites, the rest of us idiot foreigners. Occasionally chipping into my remarks about the way Soviets thought, Silvia would flare up: "Wha-a-a-t? What rubbish! In Moscow it's been a long time since that kind of thing went on," and there followed a long and condescending didactic explanation for idiot foreigners about what, why, and how things are done in Moscow. Her "you've forgotten what it's like" or "it's all changed long ago" echoed like a refrain throughout the evening.

Every now and then she would fetch more wine to fill the glass of her compatriot, each time getting up off the carpet and walking over me to get at a bottle. It was the barest of provocations: her skirt rode up and her dark mound flashed before my eyes, showing through her panties. "I forgot how curly your pubic hair was," I said, to tell her adored new arrival what our relationship was. "I keep telling you, you've been totally anglicized, you've forgotten everything," she said. "But are your legs still as hairy?" I asked, making a crude grab at her tights. I wanted the world to know about her hairy legs, and to find out if she had shaved them, to put her on the spot before her new paramour. If she had, it meant that this dope from Moscow had already slept with her, because it was something she did every time she took aboard a new lover. She blushed, either insulted and enraged, or because she guessed what I was thinking. "No hairier than your chest," she said, biting her lips. "Come on, let's compare," I replied, unknotting my tie. Without taking her eyes off me she began removing her tights.

"You Russians are always claiming the rights of the first born," Joan remarked at that point. I liked her for that, I must have been the only one to notice the reference to Jacob usurping the place of the hairy Esau. And she was the only one to understand what I meant when I said, "I prefer rootless cosmopolitanism to the Soviet electoral system." We looked knowingly at one another. At that moment she got up to go because her taxi had arrived, so I took the chance to accompany her home.

That was how our affair began, from that taxi ride across the enormous city. I tried to tell her about me and Silvia. What is gossip if not evidence of human modesty? We are afraid to talk about ourselves so we gossip about others. If the gossip intrigues the person you are talking to it shows magnanimity, sympathy, and a readiness to share experience. It reveals how willing you are to see something new in life, and tales about people you don't know very well are evidence of fellow-feeling with the person relating the gossip. In fact, when the subject of a story is scarcely known to the listener, it is gossip no longer but literature. It is like the wafer transformed into the body of Our Lord, I ventured. "Transubstantiation," she said, and our talk slid away into the charlatan metaphysics of the double meaning, where the unspoken ideas of my Soviet approach fused with her Catholicism.

My New Year's efforts did produce one result, though. The very next day Silvia rang me up and created a scene on the telephone because of the one she claimed I had created in public, by insulting her, leaving without saying goodbye, shamelessly slamming the door, and so on. I told her I hadn't slammed the door. The last time I had slammed the door was when I left Russia, on which occasion nobody had noticed me leave. "Your carryings-on with your non-existent Russian past simply made me feel sick," said I, allusively referring to her Moscow lover. "And it made me sick to watch your own carryings-on with a fictitious English present—that phoney Joanie prude," she said, not bothering with allusions. "Gotcha!" I thought with a malicious joy. "Non-existent past, fictitious present, you and your phoney new ideas," she went on, "your fictitious thinking. You dream up ideas and motives that are in practice completely unreal. Words and events that have never really existed. Your problem is not so much that your words don't match your deeds, but that your ideas don't match your words."

It is amazing how such categories can be manipulated in quarrels: whatever one says becomes the truth. "In fact you have an Othello complex, your jealousy feeds off your idle fancies. So I am sentimental about people from my past, about people who used to have a cause," she admitted. "His face hasn't changed, that was what I saw in him. Okay, he must have changed but I haven't seen him for ten years and I'd forgotten what he looked like, who he'd left me for and when. But you are always hanging around me, and you keep on going off with someone else right before my eyes. Your greatest treachery is to have changed." She was unwilling to admit that it was she who had changed. When someone changes they feel guilty about those who have remained the same. So they accuse them of having changed, of treachery. "You've changed," insisted her voice down the phone, "you've lost that sense of personal tragedy and have become simply irritable. Right before my eyes, you've turned from Othello into Iago." "Which saves you from a dreadful fate," I said, "so it won't be me who suffocates you under a pillow."

"Our Silvia is like the Soviet system; with her nobody is indispensable," I told Joan, describing Silvia's spiritual past as a striking example of how to be a chameleon and intellectual conformist while radiating the appearance of a dissident to outsiders. She was a dissident when all the Moscow elite pretended to be dissidents, she got baptized when religion was the intellectual thing to do, she emigrated when the same elite, now disillusioned, turned its face to the West and here she was, changing as fast as she could in the opposite direction, towards Russia. By leaping into Moscow's fond embrace she was rejecting me. Through her, Moscow was again expelling me beyond its frontiers, in Joan's direction.

At the same time she was changing her spiritual biography, too. In Moscow we had gone around in the same crowd, the causes and timing of our flight abroad had been more or less identical; but whenever she came back from Moscow she had a slightly altered past. She began to filter out interesting ideas to the public. She made it seem that, unlike me, she may have disagreed with the political regime, but not with the country itself. So, with the liberalization of the Soviet system she did not have much compunction about going back to Moscow. She hadn't left of her own accord; if she hadn't actually been banished, then at least she'd been squeezed out. Whereas I had left of my own accord, so to go back would have meant admitting my moral bankruptcy. Thus she turned herself into a thorough patriot while making me a rootless cosmopolitan. And as usual she was experiencing these revolutionary transformations and spiritual rebirths at just the right time: when Russia was becoming so fashionable in England.

My allegations about Silvia were so unrestrained and fanatical that the atmosphere became electric, and I produced a mesmeric effect on Joan. She seemed to warm to me. I may have been simply defending myself from cross-examination by being overly talkative, and by being frank about my Moscow past and my London reputation. But I wrongly interpreted this worldly interrogation and the subconscious suspicion lurking in it as an attempt to move in, almost like falling in love or love at first sight. In the drunken idiocy of our first intimate conversation, there was some feeling of spiritual risk, the adrenalin of opening up to a stranger that can easily be mistaken for mutual infatuation. In fact all that united us was a shared feeling of rejection.

In her own confessions to me the main subject was a case of unrequited love. For her lover's part, love seemed to be carefully divided into two parts, family and passion. Joan claimed the passion for herself, but the rest went to the crazy wife, the spoiled and cantankerous kids, and their huge mortgaged house in some remote but elegant suburb of London, which made the map of love unusually complicated. It is amazing with what stubbornness the English spend half their lives striving for complete personal independence and endeavoring to live far from the vulgar crowd, from friends they are sick of and from boring relatives, only to spend the other half going mad from the loneliness and claustrophobia of family life. She never mentioned the name of her great lover on the grounds of family security, which was a bit absurd since the wife was perfectly aware of his goings-on with Joan. I gained the impression that both the wife and Joan tried to stop talk circulating about their beloved, even as they were stoking the fires of gossip. A year ago a fateful change had occurred in the emotional triangle which was still a mystery for Joan herself, I gathered.

Not long before the cricket match I had been present during one of the "urgent" telephone calls that Joan regularly received from her lover's legal spouse. She had gone pale and biting her lips, kept saying over and over again, as if she was trying to squeeze herself into the receiver: "How awful! My God, how awful!" Afterwards, dropping into an armchair after a long pause (which I did not know how to interrupt and she did not want to), she finally revealed all to me. "A third person has come between us." That was what her lover's wife had told her, as a messenger announces to an ally that enemy forces are mustering on some distant frontier. The disaster was that the husband was in love with someone else. I saw this "disaster" and the mysterious nature of the "third person" in this soap opera of hers as the true reason she had not wanted to join me at the cricket match.

The more entangled the web of obstacles preventing the lovers from union, the more insistent were my intermittent impulses to usurp his place between her sheets. Our Dostoyevskian melodrama got heavier with every meeting: suicide threats by the wife alternated with fear of losing access to the children; he kept his geographical distance from Joan to be closer to her in spirit; he would appear at Joan's place to express compassion for the wretched, miserable, and despised—meaning his wife, Joan's complementary opposite. He would deliberately offend Joan so as to arouse her hatred, to set her free, but as soon as a final break seemed inevitable he would reappear, reopening once more the "unhealing wound of sex," to use her words. In telling me this, with a swift movement she would reach for my hand and squeeze it for an instant in her long fingers as if in a peculiar masonic handshake, as if acknowledging the intimacy of our conversations, my spiritual generosity, and my ability to understand and forgive the toils of love she was caught up in. It was almost as if I was her lover, and she was telling me about being with him. She would touch my elbow or knee as if by accident, in a sisterly manner, or take my index finger in her hand and twist it round and round like a button as we talked. She did not spurn my advances but evaded them, deflecting my every attempt to move from touching to holding. "Oh no," she would say, disentangling herself from my hands at the last moment, "it begins with kissing, but where does it all end?" And she used her own slang word in reply: insertion. She might just as well have used the words introduction or mounting. In the agreed text of our intimacy she was against unintended insertions.

These false gestures of mental intimacy, close friendship, and sisterly trust drove me to despair. She had all the tricks of a gymnast. Once, while gabbling about her entanglement she began to change to go out, to attend some function, party, or the like—and it did not enter her head to take me along, for the occasion would be another area of intimacy, another club with different confidantes. She kept up the pretense that I was her selfless admirer, close friend, faithful knight, and kindred spirit. She took a dress out of the cupboard and removed what she was wearing, to try it on before my very eyes. Undoing her bra she turned her back to me for the sake of conventional decency. She was standing before the mirror on her wardrobe door, but the door was opened in my direction. Undressing and pulling the dress over her head, she continued her inspired chirruping about the toils of love with the married monster, looking straight into my eyes in the mirror, with her body totally reflected in it. While my lips responded in a complex echo to the writhings of her soap-opera script (in which husband is won away from stupid wife), my eyes could not tear themselves away from her toy-like breasts that were in such striking contrast to her generous hips. In contemplating this naive striptease I think I was supposed to pretend that all I could see in the mirror were her lips and eyes. But again and again she would call on me directly to appraise this or that dress, skirt or accessory, while scarcely covering her nakedness and staying entangled in our absurd exchanges on the latest Jesuitical move of her tirelessly inventive lover and his ability to find yet another excuse to evade the duties of the flesh for the sake of unavoidable family obligations.

"Family life is like life under the Soviet system: in its deathly stagnation words are greater than deeds," I said, averting my gaze from the mirror and uttering the usual carefully-honed truism on the hopeless tangle of her banal little tale of unrequited love. "He is all talk and no action, he means one thing and implies another." I fixed my gaze on the delightful curve of her spine where it gave way to the hollow of her backside that peeped out over her pants. "Stalin, incidentally, reckoned that there was no such thing as thoughts without words; so every intended deed had to be formulated in words. It was important for the Great Linguist and Father of the People to show that anti-Soviet thoughts were *ipso facto* anti-Soviet propaganda." Here I was deliberately throwing dust in her eyes in order to hide the lustful gaze in my own; in recompense I was delivering her my prepackaged concept of Russian ambiguity and doublethink, while concealing my contempt for the notorious and utterly boring English hypocrisy of her banal adulterer. It flattered her: a run-of-the-mill affair with a married man became a metaphysical symbol of a split personality. Whereas I was flattered by the notion that through our foolish little intimacies I was joining, albeit vicariously, the select minority of those who could be considered true Englishmen.

These latter were a small clique of snobs who imagined they were living in the Edwardian era, before the decline of

Empire, the immigration of Pakistanis, feminism, and bans on smoking in public places. They traipsed around in a pack between three or four private clubs and pubs in Soho and were totally unapproachable. They would greet me through clenched teeth, acknowledging my presence with a nod of the head rather than a glance, and then only because once or twice when I had been with Joan she had greeted them with an exalted "Darling!", kissing each of them damply in turn, with a wave of the hand introducing me as "my Russian confidant, Zinik, you know . . . from Moscow." Again Zinik from Moscow. I had not been in Moscow for 15 years. I stood apart from them and envied them their manner of speaking that distinct and slippery English, delivered in that confused high-speed style for which they scarcely needed to open their mouths.

Sometimes my English is worse than it need be, not because I don't know the language but because I find it hard to convey the impression of an Englishman at home in his own tongue. Just as I cannot sleep with a woman without having a complete image of her, without totally imagining that I have already slept with her. That is, a language is like being with a girl friend: either you sleep with her or she is not your girl friend. Whereas you can still be close to a wife without going to bed with her.

At that time my relationship to English was that of man and wife, and it was an unaccustomed feeling. Until arriving in England I could not imagine the difference between wife and mistress, so far as closeness was concerned. Joan's irritating inaccessibility also showed itself linguistically in our relationship, which had none of the incomprehensible stutters and jerks that distinguish one's mother tongue from one that has been learned, or mark old acquaintances off from close friends and distinguish friends from lovers. I failed to understand this and instead would get caught up in wordy knots, making my thoughts complicated and hoping that the resultant surreal effect would bring me by winding byways to the hot and trembling essence of Joan's being, to her damp "unhealing wound" and the defencelessness that underlay the dry and leathery skin of her forty-year-old worldliness. In the endlessly unwinding conversation of hers I began to drink more and more (she taught me to drink whisky, diluting it with water in the English fashion) and every time we met we would more or less sink a bottle of Famous Grouse. My hand would wander from her shoulder to knee, but just when I was about to take the decisive step into an intimacy of pose and position she would come out with her classical phrase about "insertion" and throw me out. I would leave early in the morning exhausted and deaf from the sound of my own words, with a ringing head and sad emptiness in my heart, still feeling triply treacherous: in thought, word, and deed.

2

From the evasive look in her eyes I guessed that she felt my presence at the cricket match was like the "insertion" she was so keen to avoid. I was from a different neck of the woods; a different text, a different test. She turned immediately, took me by the arm and launched on her indiscriminate stylized "daahling" routine, introducing me to her friends with ill-concealed nervousness, reacting each time with panic and surprise when she noticed that most of them already knew me (as an author) and I did not need to be introduced. Like an entertainer who tries to hide after a second-rate cabaret number she dragged me to the bar in the marquee away from the cricket pitch and behind the spectators' deck chairs. From her shifting stare and constant circling on the spot, it was clear that the problem was not her confusion at catching sight of me. She was obviously looking for someone. It was not hard to guess who.

"Darling," she called out to yet another unknown individual standing at the bar. For all the affectation in her greeting, her voice conveyed an exaggerated carelessness, an almost coy irony; yet her fingers clung to the palm of my hand in a deathly grip, like the cramped grasp of someone drowning. He was just as I had imagined. Though with his children and crazy wife, he might have been expected to look older still. Even so, despite his comparative youth and athletic appearance, there was a slight alcoholic puffiness about his face and the bags under his eyes made it harder to guess his age, though not his social standing in our tiny world. He seemed a parody of everything Joan had conjured up as the image of an Englishman: those grey whiskers and port-wine cheeks, that network of blood vessels on them underscored by his particolored tie, his whole visual effect seeming specially tailored to match his striped summer suit with its green Oscar Wilde carnation in his lapel. His external appearance was more important than the man, and his words were more important than his ideas. I guessed at an inimitable quick-fire delivery, insulting in its incomprehensibility to an outsider. But here I did not consider myself an outsider, so I examined him with curiosity.

"Pimm's?" he said, turning to Joan, demonstratively ignoring me while managing to look so condescending that I thought he used the word "pimps". He evidently considered me one of Joan's hangers-on. Turning his back to me, he reached out to pass a brim-full glass to her, swayed slightly and almost spilled the drink on my sleeve. He was evidently no longer sober.

Joan tried to smooth over his rudeness, shoving me forward as if I were an infant. "Zinik, my Russian, you know," she began again in her usual hateful recitation. His name was

Ricketts. Irritated, I burst out: "I haven't been a Russian for a long time now," like a child whose talents are being excessively praised before dinner guests. This time, however, the grown-up ignored me. He merely raised his eyebrows and leaned across the bar for his whisky and water, almost elbowing me aside. There was nothing for it but to order a Pimm's for myself. "With cucumber," I added loudly, for his benefit and to show him I too knew what people in England drank with their cucumbers. But they had run out. "Orange, in that case," said I, but suddenly panicked: cucumber yes, but orange? Following the barman with my eyes as he nimbly sliced the orange into segments, I noticed it was from Israel—a Jaffa. "But I have a British passport: I pledged my allegiance to the Queen," I said. Solely for Joan's sake, and in an attempt to strike up a conversation with the monster she was in love with: in order to press her suit with him she clearly needed either a go-between or witness, a Third Man or superfluous hero.

"Why are all your lovers such impossible little liars?" sneered this terrible man through clenched teeth.

"He's not my lover," said Joan.

"But he is an impossible little liar." They were already scoring points off one another as if I didn't exist. Ricketts swayed on his heels and, without turning his head, as if he had lumbago or a crick in his neck, swung his whole frame round at me. "Who the hell are you? Where do you come from? What are you doing here?" He shook with anger and spots appeared on his already flushed cheeks. He was much taller than me and from where I stood the Windsor knot in his brightly colored tie appeared to underpin his chin, seeming to force it backwards and increasing the effect of his supercilious grimace. "What can cricket mean to you? You're a foreigner, why are you here? It's a foolish English game. It isn't a game, it's a form of torture. We used to get caned if we skipped a match. On the backside, on the bare bum, our trousers down! That's what cricket means to us! But what is it to you? I can't see what brought you. Who did bring you, anyway?"

"You know very well who asked him to come," Joan burst in.

"Our Arthur and his strange penchant for intellectuals of doubtful political convictions from all sorts of stinking foreign parts. His pathological proclivity for ethnic exotica, no doubt. Or is it his conscience at our former empire—colonies and small nations?"

"Are Russians a small nation? Is Russia a former colony? Whose colony? What are you saying? Come on, let's leave now," said Joan tugging at his sleeve.

"He's not from Russia. What's Russia got to do with it? We know all about your lot now," he said, addressing me, completely ignoring Joan. "I've read all your grand works about the Iron Curtain and all that. So long as you were hiding behind a tatty old curtain you could say you were anybody. A Russian or a Tartar, anybody. But the Iron Curtain has collapsed. Your cover is blown, comrade, you've been exposed for the charlatan you are. The whole damn charade!" His sharp hysterical baritone began attracting looks from every side. I felt the burning heat of the air trapped under the stuffy tarpaulin of the marquee. The sunlight seeped through the white tarpaulin as if bringing to heat up together an ominous alchemy of the different colored liquors in the bottles ranged behind the bar, which threw a bilious reflection on to his face already shiny with sweat. His moist lips trembled like those of a horse flicking off flies with its tail. "You really think he's a Russian, Joanie?" he asked her with a crooked grin. "Joanie, he's a horrible little liar. He's not a Russian. He's not a Brit. He's a Jew, Joanie. You are a Jew-boy, aren't you?" he repeated, with a scarcely perceptible sneer, and the word crawled out of his twisted mouth like a slippery fat worm. I noticed a kind of no-man's-land forming around us: the crowd of gentlemen gathered round the middle of the bar were carefully melting away. "You're no Russian, my friend, with your Jewish ideas, and you're no Brit, with your Russian tricks. You're a nobody!"

"But I've still got my Israeli passport," I said, coming back at him with self-deprecating humor. Fool that I was, I still hoped to reduce his nonsensical rudeness to a drunken joke, if only one in bad taste. "So I am not only a Russian Jew, I am also a British Israelite. To misquote Nabokov, the Neptune of all three waves of Russian emigration: my brain is Russian, my heart is English, and my soul is Jewish."

"Heart and soul, soul and . . . liver. What nationality is your liver? Or your genitals? What do you use to break the bones of Palestinian youths in the territories occupied by your circumcised soul? And who does it owe its allegiance to, King David? Or who?" He wiped the palm of his hand on his thighs and knees, as a bowler will sometimes wipe the cricket ball on his trouser legs, before running up to the stump and bowling it at the batsman.

"I don't live in the territories and I have not broken anyone's bones. At least not so far." I averted my gaze, and instead concentrated on attempting to extract the segment of Israeli orange which I tried to remove from the English stewed fruit in its tight little glass. "Anyhow, what about you? Where is it you come from, then?" My hands trembled; the piece of orange wouldn't come out.

"From the end of the line. Nowhere else to go. Or emigrate to. Nowhere. There are Jewish intellectuals everywhere, like you. I don't like Jewish intellectuals." He turned sharply away, jogging my shoulder, and strode off, dragging Joan after him. The orange segment chose that moment to jump out from between my fingers, slip out of the glass, and drop onto the ground. I bent straight down to pick it up, embarrassed at my clumsiness, though to look at me people might have thought I was bowing down before the impertinent Ricketts, who was now disappearing into a shaft of sunlight blinding the exit. After a while, a great sigh of collective disappointment rose from outside: the batsman had either not hit the ball far enough, or it had been caught by one of the fielders. After a while the click of ball on bat recommenced. Like a champagne bottle being opened at a party you are not invited to.

As I left the marquee I was greeted by a liquid clapping from the spectators. The way a spoon will ring in a glass of tea, or when a horse is tapped on its crupper. Yet the spectators continued to talk to their friends. The supercilious applause, almost wrung out of them, was not aimed at me, though it did apply to my situation: it was directed at a batsman run out and sent off the field. The applause was ironic: the worse the batsman played during his innings, the louder the clapping. The latest batsman dismissed can't have been too bad, and he came bearing down on me in his whites with their high shin-pads like an angel or knight of old, armed with a bat instead of a lance. His entire right side had been spattered with mud, though I had taken the cricket pitch to be a seamless silken greensward.

After the half-light of the bar tent the searing sunlight hammered into my brain. Like an actor blundering about in the wings, who suddenly finds himself pushed on stage, I sought out my former drinking companion. Arthur had just risen from his deck chair, continuing to sneeze into his handkerchief, but the picture of misery was shattered by the fact that as he stood up his eyes were searching feverishly around. Our gaze met and I was about to head in his direction, when with a sudden and unexpected rudeness he waved me away as if I was some irritating fly. He ambled off towards the entrance to the ground, where Joan could be seen catching hold of her bowler hat with one hand while assisting the far from sober Ricketts with the other. Arthur was evidently trying to catch up with them. It was not clear why: I flattered myself he was intending to remonstrate with Ricketts for his outrageous behavior. His prominent shoulder blades shook beneath his white jacket.

I collapsed into his deck chair. The hum of conversation that resumed around me could not entirely drown the crickety-click of insults burning through my head. The reptile teaches me the difference between a Jew, a Tartar, and a nobody. "Who do you take yourself for? You're a nobody!" Sorry. I may be simply translating from one language to another but my intent is artistic. I am a man of the arts. I take myself for nobody but myself alone. The first prerequisite of an artist is to be nobody. I have already sold out my country. All I have left to sell is myself. But I can't make a sale. Solitude and craftsmanship. And some third thing too, according to Joyce, who had every right to hold his wake for Finnegan amid the Swiss cows; and Muriel Spark was fully entitled to spend her days idling among French peasant women. So why should I, of the Moscow Komsomol, have to stay in the USSR without a murmur and provide the decadent West with a moral example of forbearance deep in the Siberian mines?

Still maddened with rage, I ran through the list of stinging rejoinders I might have made. There was that haughty nonentity, Ricketts. I knew all there was to know about him, didn't I? I might have humiliated him with references to his hysterical wife and bitchy daughters. Or taken my glass of that English version of Russian cold soup and hurled it in his face, and watched him with satisfaction as he tried to remove the Israeli orange peel caught in his hair. At all events why should I let the insult go unavenged? How witty, cold-blooded, and murderously precise I might have been in my reply to this spoiled slob. When he said he couldn't abide Jewish intellectuals, I should have replied: "Unfortunately, there I can't help you." Of course he would have misunderstood me, he wouldn't have known how I could have helped in other respects. I would have paused exactly the right length of time and said: "You don't like Jews? That's your problem. You're mentally disturbed. You're suffering from a seriously disordered brain. Go see your doctor. Or a psychoanalyst. You need treatment. I can't help you." Then I would have turned and swaggered elegantly towards the pitch to watch the final minutes of the game. Solitude and craftsmanship. And cricket. But the match was already superfluous to my needs.

3

The cricket pitch and the white outlines of the players on their flat green background, the spectators laid low by the heat in their deck chairs, all seemed to be out of focus. I felt it occupied some singularity in space-time, a repeated disharmony; the bowlers with the endless swinging of their arms before they bowled, the batsman defending his wicket, constantly throwing his leg forward and bending it at the knee, and repeatedly hitting the invisible ball into the air. The umpire, the arbiter, in his white coat and his equally white visored hat, for all the world like an orderly in a mental hospital, regarded his patients with condescending equanimity. With the fanaticism of the insane the maniacs under his charge kept gathering into little huddles and exploding in different directions or freezing into complete immobility before hurling themselves at one another again. In an obvious attempt to dampen the aggressive tendencies of these schizophrenics at play, the umpire would occasionally wave at them, with threatening gestures comprehensible only to the lunatics gamboling before him.

A mysterious interplay of gestures that a minute before had seemed completely clear to me, now made my gaze blur over with the clinical alienation of a mirage in the desert. Only instead of desert dunes the sleek shaven cricket pitch gleamed like the sweaty hide of some monster. The wondrous grassy mattress of an unnatural green may have been no more than an arm's length away but it was still unattainable. It had taken such an effort of mind to reach this oasis in the desert of English alienation. I had begun to consider the cricket pitch my own. It was to have been my sky, my green. And my cricket match. I had unraveled the secret of its beauty, I had grasped it, I had made it my own. But abruptly I had been given to realize that comprehension alone was not enough. Understanding and belonging were not identical. Relationship does not convey the feeling of own-ness, of belonging to a club. To our cricket club. Instead, it is a club you will never be admitted to. In an instant, a few half-drunken insults had made me lose the temporarily acquired feeling of belonging to a new country. I knew for certain I would never again feel I belonged to it. So far as my former country was concerned, all I remembered was that I had once wanted to win myself a place there, but now the desire refused to return. It was like a momentary glimpse of old age: when you remember the wonderful state of being in love but know it will never happen again, yet you still remember that you once wanted to want. I left the cricket ground.

Once inside the heavy cast-iron door of an old-style telephone box, as red as a pioneer's neckerchief, I dialed Silvia's number. But scarcely had I heard her familiar hoarse voice answer than I remembered we were no longer talking to one another, and hung up, leaving the receiver dangling. There was nobody left to ring. In all of London with its roaring din of endless acquaintances, the only confidante left to me had been Silvia. Only with Silvia might I have been able to conjure away the strange metamorphosis that had come over me a quarter of an hour earlier. Only with Silvia could I really have discussed how much I missed her. But she was far away, dreadful treachery on her part. "Do something to make me stop hating you because it is you I love," I muttered at myself through clenched teeth. I felt sick. That trash with cucumbers and orange peel I had consumed was making itself known, in my legs if not in my head.

Unsteady of leg, I knew exactly where the turn of events was leading me. To Soho, to any establishment where I might run into Joan. The brazen-faced Ricketts had carried her off, Joan the only woman I could talk to now, Joan who was the only one I could talk to about Silvia's part in my life, about how I could change my habits of a lifetime and find another way of being. The two of them, Joan and Silvia, were assuming a dialectical unity and I could not disentangle them. But there was no room in this subdivision for a third person, an unnecessary encumbrance like the awful Ricketts. Yet it was Ricketts' face I caught myself seeking in the crowd, in the hope that Joan would be with him. In their haunts round Old Compton Street my searching eye became confused; now and then I would stumble across her likeness with the same thickly coated eyelashes, the same plucked eyebrows, the same blood-red lipstick and deathly pale skin shaded by her russet fringe and the bowler hat she had been wearing, the same fishnet tights and absurdist decadence of lace and plush flounces. Girls of her type multiplied like tadpoles in a pond with every pub I looked into on the way to Dean Street, and the manner-ist eclecticism of their dress garnered from every age turned this corner of London into a time machine that buzzed and danced on the spot: was it the thirties? The fifties? The turn of the century? And if so, what century?

One of these women, who must have been drunk from early morning, grabbed hold of me when at last I ended up at the French Pub, a demonstratively shabby joint on which Joan descended every once in a while. Before reaching it I had looked in at Groucho's, where the wealthier Bohemians gathered, where I had not been permitted beyond the foyer; I had glanced inside the Coach and Horses on the corner of Greek Street, where the punters pretend to be drinking but are actually waiting to get an eyeful of Jeffrey Barnard and to eavesdrop on his joyously pessimistic alcoholic philosophy. I even ventured into the Green Room at the Colony, where people may look as if they are talking but in fact cram into it in the hope of sighting Francis Bacon. As recently as that same morning I would still have pictured myself as being at home among all those improbable faces, faces you would never encounter in other London establishments. They were all sworn friends of Joan, and I felt a vicarious sense of belonging to that weird human zoo, with those staccato gestures and false intonations, twisted features and alcoholic deviations: they seemed like a bunch of aristocratic eccentrics in a circus ring, and since I too was an alien monster from some other planet, their artificial surroundings made flesh and conscious deformity had until now created a sensation of almost domestic comfiness, different from the external world of public affluence. I had imagined I was on the point of joining their number. Yet the day's events had shown me that the crowd had its own passport system, and that entry to the kingdom was barred for me; the best I could hope for was a short-stay tourist visa permitting me to visit it as an outsider.

The habitués of these places, measuring me up with a glance, acknowledged my appearance with a scarcely perceptible nod of the head, and when I asked if Joan had been in, they either emitted evasively polite affirmatives or exalted and pretentious remarks as if we were at some worldly gathering of the best society: "Joan? Of course! Joan! You're a friend of Joan's. Of course, dear boy, over here from Muscovy, aren't you? A real Russian. Here for long? Come here to visit us in Albion, have you?" And for the umpteenth time I barked out that I'd been here for fifteen years, in a fury wrenching myself away from the made-up monstereen with lilac nails, who clung to my jacket flaps at the bar of the French Pub.

My outburst shattered the drowsy afternoon spell hanging over the place. At this time of day, the bar was half empty and caught by shafts of dusty sunlight, stuck in a time warp going back to the fifties, the last time the place had been redecorated. Its interior had absolutely nothing remarkable about it. I was always lost for words at its style, or rather lack of style, because it was the personal style of the particular group of customers gathered there at any given time, and no more. An object frozen in time loses its name, because in describing things we do not give them names of their own but name them in the light of whimsical associations, allusions and recollections of our own times, unlike the way we name people. That barroom and stuffy little entrance hall, which had fallen into the present from out of its own times, was like an archaeological curiosity. The gloomy mix of wall-paint, dark green and brown, almost straight out of a painting by Rembrandt, formed a tasteless contrast with the variety posters from unknown years and clown-like photos of well-known figures who had been friends of the owner or customers. They shamelessly compared the incomparable, with this elementary eclecticism lending a kind of charm to the place. It was not so much a style as the impress of a way of thinking, a way of life. And the way of life was not my own, and the words I could use did not fit. I had never belonged to that period and could not feel sentimental about it as a vanished time. There was a smell of sour wine, dirty linoleum, and cigar smoke. The few customers in the pub were leaning up against the bar in the afternoon sunlight as if caught in a picture frame, and I was regarding them from two yards away like a visitor to a museum. I stood immobile and my previous outburst only served to underscore my silence in those surroundings. Just then, I saw a hand waving in greeting from a far corner of the bar. It seemed to volunteer assistance in asserting my right to live in these islands.

"Would you care to join me?" said Arthur Simons from his corner, dragging over a free chair. It was obvious why I had not immediately picked him out: his tie was at half-mast like the union jack in a time of mourning, his shoulders were slumped and I detected on his cheeks a stubble uncharacteristic in one who was always so clean-shaven. "I suspect we are looking for the same persons," he said, and he raised his eyes to me, eyes as colorless as the drink in the narrow glass standing before him. He added that he had tried phoning Joan but with no success. The phone was as dead as a doornail. Then he blew his nose again, diving down into his handkerchief as if mourning the dead, but the weepiness of the hay fever victim had become a bout of feverish consumption, his eyelids red as if after a night's lost sleep.

"How did the match finish?" he asked, twisting his glass in his hands. I said I had been unable to watch to the end because of that brazen individual with whom I had my own unsportsmanlike score to settle. "Pay no attention to Ricketts' rudeness, dear boy," he said, with a grimace of exhaustion as if he was already completely in the picture about what had happened at the bar in the cricket-ground marquee. "He was dead drunk. Wouldn't hurt a fly. A tender soul, believe me." When I started telling him of Ricketts' boorishness, Arthur came to life: "Look, his anti-Semitic outbursts are only linguistic games, believe you me. I've shown him your Otto Weininger piece. He was quoting you back at yourself. Out of the mouths of others, one's own ideas always sound insulting. He thinks he's some kind of Weininger himself. What can you expect from a second-generation Catholic? He comes from a family of German Jewish converts. Like any hidden Jew he can't stand his own past. But you're right about one thing; he was looking for an excuse to insult you. He found your sore point, and it was one he knew from his own experience."

"Unlike Weininger, so far as I can see, his sore points cover a lot of ground. He's extremely good at passing on a feeling of self-loathing to his near ones and dear ones. He's brought his wife almost to the point of suicide, he will turn his children into parricides, unless Joan does him in first, or before his tender-heartedness gets her thrown into a nut house."

"What has Joan told you about *my* family situation? That all my family worries are due to her?"

"What's your family situation got to do with it? I'm talking about Ricketts."

"You may not know, dear fellow, but it is my wife who has the suicide complex. As do our children. But Joan has nothing to do with the matter. Though we did once have a brief fling. That was when I was still trying to be interested in women." He looked searchingly into my eyes as if trying to gauge my reaction. "Until the moment my wife thought the triangle with Joan was permanent and would not bend. I didn't try to enlighten her. Triangle there may have been, but it was of a different shape." He slowed down. "As for being latent. For some reason in your piece on Weininger you never mentioned that he was a latent homosexual too. And Ricketts is far from latent."

"Are you telling me he was just another spare prick?" I grimaced in a stupid and helpless smile.

"You do realize, don't you, that he was not jealous of you because of Joan?" he continued after a pause, "but because of me. I was watching him when you and I were discussing cricket at the edge of the pitch. He's been in a dreadful state for the past two months, ever since the death of a mutual . . . friend . . . of ours." He again plunged his face weepily into his handkerchief as if hiding from inquisitive stares. "People are dying like flies. It's his Jewish streak at work; he's observing the mourning period to the very last. It takes a special form with him: he doesn't eat at all and every day half drinks himself to death. He rings up in the middle of the night. He's rude to outsiders. You know what it's like to have a completely apocalyptic attitude to things—there is never a shortage of evidence to prove you're right. I promised to spend the whole day with him and to leave the match once it was under way. But he began drinking in the morning. Apart from everything else, with my hay fever I wasn't feeling up to much and we had a row over his drunken hysterics. And then Joan exploited his jealousy by taking him away from me. To take it out on me. It wasn't you she was getting at. Not at all. She never even thought you would turn up at the match."

Indeed, I should never have gone to it at all, if only to have avoided all these sensational revelations, the gravest of which showed me up as a typical foreign idiot, ready to be manipulated by anyone who felt up to it.

"So what will you drink?" he said slapping my knee soothingly and raising a finger to attract the owner's attention, an ancient charmer called Gaston, calling him *garçon* with drunken abandon; but Gaston, with his luxuriant handlebar mustache melting away into his sideburns, was kissing the hand of a peroxide blonde, who looked as if she had stepped out of the Moulin Rouge in some Toulouse-Lautrec cartoon. "You think Gaston is kissing her hand? In fact he is wiping his mustache on her. Like cats lick their fur. He claims to be a Frenchman, but he isn't really. He's Flemish. The Flemings are well-known for their meanness. I've known him for twenty years and not once in all that time has he offered me a drink."

Arthur tapped the table with his empty glass. I took the

hint and asked him what he wanted. "The same again, dear boy, a Ricard. *Garçon, deux pastis s'il vous plait. Deux Ricards, vous comprenez?*" Gaston smiled into his mustache with idiotic geniality, obviously not quite understanding what was wanted. Arthur switched to English. "His phoney French," he muttered at the retreating back, "like our Joan's pseudo-aristocratic manner of speech. The French always have that childish lisp when they switch to English; it's because they can't purse their lips."

"Switch? Joan? From what language?" I didn't understand.

"How do you mean from what? From French of course. Didn't you know?" And for the first time in the conversation he smiled. And the more I went on to hear, the more contented I felt: like a betrayed husband who has practically found his wife a lover, to give himself grounds for a divorce. With a strange easing of the spirit like the final defeat in a ghastly war, I listened to Arthur as he proceeded to inform me in his dry legalistic voice that, actually, my ideal English rose had been born in the French provinces, in one of those demi-suburbs stretching between Amiens and Paris, in some small town smelling of death and right thinking. From which any truly right-thinking individual would be bound to flee, as from the Soviet system. She had escaped in the sixties immediately on leaving school. According to Arthur, she had flattered her snobby London associates with her Frenchness, though my untrained ear had been unable to catch the coquettish lisp, her fixed smile, and her general airs, which I considered the purest English chic, had taken me in completely.

"Joan. Jeanne. Our own Joan of Arc," he went on. "The clumsy way she had of dressing, like a Victorian prostitute, imagining in her naiveté that it was the way Virginia Woolf might have dressed. The pitifully mendacious snobbishness that made her include the area round King's Cross as part of

Bloomsbury. Only a foreigner can so equivocate. You know, dear boy, she's from a family of French Huguenots. The Huguenots fled to England from the Catholics. But there were English Catholics who fled in the opposite direction, to France. To be a Catholic in England is more fashionable— after all they are what you would call dissidents over there in Moscow, so Joan immediately said she was a Catholic. It's as if an Englishman arrived in Moscow, you know, and immediately began to wear a Jewish *kaftan* and *yarmolka*, with a scroll of the Torah in one hand and a fiddle in the other. I'm not surprised that Ricketts, with his Jewish ancestors, who imagines himself to be a true Catholic, thinks she's a spiritual charlatan. I can't understand how he allowed her to take him away from the cricket ground; he is sickened by her goings-on. But a shared thirst for revenge, dear boy, outweighs any feeling of mutual alienness, don't you think?"

Every word he uttered made me feel more and more brotherly towards Joan. I was not some monster from another planet, after all. I was not alone. If need be, I could melt back into a crowd of people who were kindred beings. Everything I had taken as irksome inaccessibility was rather a shared feeling of alienation about the language that we communicated in. "I can't imagine how your Russian ear could have failed to pick up her French accent," smiled Arthur. "You know, she always confused an innocent enough swear word like 'bugger' with the word 'beggar' and so she's always been convinced the English hate down-and-outs. Your Russian Alexander Herzen always thought so too, unless I'm mistaken. There is some similarity, old chap, between you and the French in your careless disregard of English phonetics." I was about to say I was not Russian but experience caused me to keep my peace. Joan and I were birds of a feather. We may have been rotten apples but we were from the same barrel. "That Russian and French conviction that all Englishmen are queers. In any case I'm almost convinced, dear boy, that she has suspected you and me of being lovers. Perhaps my wife gave her that idea. Which means she may have been playing not only on Ricketts' jealousy of me because of you, but on my jealousy of you because of Ricketts. But that would have been a trifle complicated for her Gallic temperament to work out, wouldn't it?" For an instant I felt that in laying his cards on the table like this he might have been propositioning me for a role as the superfluous man.

Just then, through the open doorway of the pub, veered the figure of Ricketts, outlined briefly in the striking pose of some theatrical tableau. But his appearance was pitiful and tortured. It was not clear where he had spent the last few hours but his parted grey hair, so carefully tended over the past years, was sticking up like the quills on a ruffled porcupine. His tie hung askew, a button had been almost torn off and was attached by a single thread from his shirtfront, which was wide open. I noticed that the infamous green carnation no longer adorned the buttonhole of his ripped lapel. He looked as if he had been in a fight. With a throaty and weepy cry he hurled himself towards Arthur, upsetting a chair and catching him in his arms like a ball in flight. I saw his shoulders heaving under his jacket.

"Welcome to the club," Arthur winked at me when at last he managed to detach himself from Ricketts, raising his glass in which the dissolved white pastis was suspended like a flag of truce. The demented Ricketts, who now aroused in me nothing more than pity, stood with his back to me without apparently noticing my presence. A few of the others at the bar also raised their glasses, as if joining in Arthur's toast. But though they were merely greeting Ricketts, who was obviously one of them, I took their gesture as an invitation to join their number, the club of those who belong to no club. I felt briefly I was of their company, but that in itself helped me refuse their offer. I could exist for myself. Which was important for me. The word was mightier than the deed. And the thought more mighty than the word.

In the late afternoon sunlight, Soho had lost its coarse and dessicated roughness, that mix of garishness and loudness, that burning desire to attract as well as to repel, that I had encountered in every bar, pub, and café just an hour before. The street was now a cozy front room, on which the doormen in the restaurants were drawing the curtains. The posters and shop fronts might have been so many pictures on the wall, and the brickwork along their façades so much wallpaper. Those who lived in this front room, from the pimps frozen in doorways to the concert ticket agents and Jewish photographers, followed me with welcoming gaze and friendly nods, not importunately, but as if they were seeing an old friend coming back home to his usual corner armchair. The street was anonymous because of that English habit of posting a street name only at each end, so you never know where you are. But I no longer needed names. I was coming home.

The way home was predictably entangled, however: the day would obviously not be complete until I saw Joan again. Her manipulations had for so long firmly shoved me onto the back burner of her personal relationships that it was surprising I was the only one left defending her wicket. Grabbing a bottle of whisky on the way, I went round to her place, imagining our meeting and reconciliation down to the finest details: her frown of surprise, slowly changing to an ill-concealed smile as we sat in her window seat watching the midsummer sunset, with me telling her everything I thought about England, three-sided love affairs, and cricket. I would tell her as I filled our glasses that even full understanding is insufficient for feeling part of something, for having the sensation of belonging to club and clan. But, while recognizing that the two feelings did not interlock, you could suddenly understand that in the whole of merry England it was not only you who did not have the feeling of truly belonging, but everyone else as well. And that, in the final analysis, she was the only superfluous hero in this story. In the same way that it would have been me if the story had a slightly different twist. And that two superfluous people could make a wonderful couple if only they could shed their former stories. While telling her this, my hands would be engaged in a totally different play, which would imperceptibly invade her whole being and take over her body. And when the story reached its climax we would arrive at the final conclusion that there is no alienation or division that cannot be moved by love.

After knocking the requisite number of times on the door (doorbells were things that Joan naturally scorned to use), I pressed my nose against the ground-floor window, without perceiving any sign of life in the darkened aquarium inside. But when I rapped on the door a second time, it began to squeak open of its own accord: Joan had probably slipped out for some cigarettes. Going down the hall I called out to her, without much hope of a reply. I found her in the living room: she had simply nodded off in front of the fireplace, oblivious to the world. The ruddy glare of the sunset reflected through the window set her face on fire, though the grate was a minia-ture one and purely decorative, the size of a wicket. Her head lay thrown back against it, and it was as if she was on a cricket pitch. The closer I came the more unnatural appeared the pose that she lay crouched in. At last I remembered to switch on the standard lamp in the corner of the room, which extinguished the light from the fiery red sky outside.

What had seemed to be sunset reflected on her face actu-ally turned out to be scratches and cuts as dark as Pimm's. She lay hunched up as if in pain, her dress torn open from throat to pubis, the ripped black lace flounces like pools of dark against her cricket-white thighs. Her nipples started out furtively, but there was no more need to pretend to notice only her eyes and lips. I put my ear close to her chest, for once and probably the last time in my life, trying to guess whether there was anyone inside trying to knock through to me. I could not hear anything, but knew that did not necessarily mean there was nothing beating. That she no longer needed translation into another language. Trying to put a pillow under her head, my fingers were smeared with the same sticky liquid that blurs the most squeaky of dénouements: the russet curls on her forehead stuck together in a heap of coarse and bloody wool. It was only then I noticed that, lying in the tiny wicket of the fireplace, there was a full-sized iron. I recalled Arthur's words about a shared thirst for revenge being stronger than a feeling of mutual alienation. He had said enough to convince me of his indifference to her. But how far had he been believed by the other protagonists in the story? Was he indeed its centerpiece? And who was really the superfluous man? Who had been the most jealous? In the world of words and deeds she still lived, but ideas were beyond her. The creature with the cracked skull lying on the green carpet had tried to vanquish her own feelings of banishment as an outsider, causing jealousy in others, unaware that she too might become its victim, that someone else might be jealous of her, or she of someone else. Alienation is a feeling that can be overcome not only by love, but by hate as well. From outside the window came the wail of a siren from a police car or an ambulance, which in all these years I had been unable to distinguish, and a squeal of brakes. As if awakened by these wails of hatred and despair, Joan moaned slightly, though not yet returning to consciousness. She was alive, all the same. Swaying, I carefully unknotted her fingers, removing from them the over-obvious yet deceptive evidence: the livid green carnation.

At that moment Silvia emerged furtively from the room

next door. "We've been having a bit of a fracas over you," she said, looking round.

We were kept at the police station till well past midnight, and in the taxi afterwards Silvia, released on bail, after not uttering a word throughout most of the journey, finally told me that her application for a visa to visit Moscow had been turned down. I said she should attach no importance to it: it could be rejected today and granted tomorrow. "That's not what I'm worried about," she said. "You know, I feel as if a whole age has passed away. It's as if I've been living in another country since last we met, another city, somewhere like Moscow." And going into her flat, she said without a break in her words, "I've shaved my legs again."

"Who's the lucky man?"

"Guess," she said and began to take off her tights. The lesson cricket teaches us is that after every run you must get back to your wicket: your bat has to reach the crease, or you might be run out. Anyhow, those are rules. That was all words. Or thoughts, without words. But I was beyond words, or thinking, for that matter.

A moment later, I saw before me again the green nap of the cricket pitch glistening damply in the sunlight, but turning and thickening in color to such a velvet darkness that I was afraid to miss the ball. I clenched my teeth and concentrated as it seemed to grow in size in front of my eyes. It bounced off my bat with a dull smacking sound, and I hit it mightily, striking straight up, far away into the sky, where it burst amid the blue like the egg yolk of the sun, its rays spraying through the heavens. And I knew that now I could make as many runs as I wanted.

1990

Translated by Bernard Meares

AN UNINVITED GUEST

NOT FOR THE FIRST TIME, I HAD CONTRIVED TO SIT OUT A
national disaster abroad. I heard about the London hurricane
on the radio, just as I was giving myself up to melancholy in a
bay of the Atlantic under a Portuguese sun. My initial reaction
to the news was a complacent smirk: what luck, being here
and not there. To hell with them and their hurricanes. Then
the mental carriage-bar shot back—what about our London
roof, and the giant chestnuts opposite? The huge old tree
outside my windows seemed to breathe its last as I thought
about it: a massive top like that, its furrowed, hollowed-
out trunk—I could picture it collapsing of its own accord
from the sheer weight of its ageing body. But I found out later
that it is these old reprobates whose roots go down scores of
feet, while those of the patriarchal and morally staunch oak
tree had spread out over the surface. The hurricane had laid
hold of its crown and turned it upside down in two seconds
flat.

A tree torn up by the roots is a dreadful sight—doubly so if
the tree is of vast size. You stand there at a loss, stunned and
ashamed; it's like seeing someone elderly fall over in the street.
It's as if you were to blame for not having leapt forward in
time and grabbed them by the elbow. Strangely enough, not
one of the toppled giants had damaged the nearby houses.
They had all fallen in the opposite direction. Evidently the
walls of the buildings had deflected the blast of the storm,
causing the trunks to be hurled away from them.

Nevertheless, not even my melancholy Atlantic retreat
could escape the gales and torrential downpour; but by then I

didn't connect that catastrophic night on the shores of the Atlantic with the hurricane in England. It's easy to shuffle the past and make it into something meaningful and symbolically significant in the light of some later disaster. Let the catastrophe happen as long as it has some edifying lesson to impart. But there was no such significance in that early autumn. It was the merest chance that had brought me to that Portuguese township on the Atlantic seaboard: Varvara von Lubeck (her family were White Russian émigrés of Baltic German baronial stock) had offered me her villa for the traditional peppercorn, because her usual summer tenants had died. For my part I agreed, because I needed to get away like a snake needs to slough its skin, though it's hard to say whether the snake actually does transform itself in the process or just wriggles out of its former wearisome situation.

That month the news of my mother's death finally reached me. According to my friends and relations, the news had arrived a month late because of the machinations of the Soviet censors. The same Soviet organs were to blame, it seemed, for the fact that it was impossible to get through to London from Moscow. When you've lived in London for a dozen years you realize that chaos in the post office or on the telephone isn't always inspired by a malignant bureaucratic system. The depressing absurdity of these belated obsequies lay in something else entirely: I had finally managed to compose a postcard to my mother—a very rare occurrence in all these years, since my relations with my parents, generally speaking, had never been established in a verbal sense. The postcard had been sent to one already dead. Still, like all émigrés, I had been deprived of Soviet citizenship and black-listed; I knew when I left Moscow that I would never see any of my close relatives again and had accordingly reconciled myself to the idea that they had already died, so to speak, as far as I was concerned. Someone who quits his homeland for ever looks on it as the beyond, "the other world" tucked away behind a gothic iron curtain. And this feeling is reciprocal: we regard those over there as living corpses. They regard us as phantoms.

The news of my mother's death did not evoke any feeling whatsoever, apart from an adolescent sense of shame at my own lack of feeling. What's more, as I recalled her face, her voice and gestures, her ways, manners, and habits, I experienced a kind of relief that I would never see them again. I would never have to witness her petty family scheming, the incredible torrent of talk and her fondness for the melodramatic gesture, her habit of interrupting everyone, her impudence and her total conviction that everyone around her was obliged to see to her wants—because of her supposedly grave bodily infirmities, which did not, however, prevent her trailing off to the four corners of the earth if she had taken it into her head to have a gossip with some old friend, or stroll round the second-hand shops to look over their bric-a-brac, of which we had enough in the house to sink a battleship. I pictured our abode: the cup of coffee masked by a brassiere, the nylon stocking used as a book-mark, her habit of eating with her fingers, the way she used to appear half-dressed at dinner time, her hair all over the place as she bent over me to tick me off for my usual boyish scruffiness, tousling her head as the hairs rained into my plate. Recalling all this, I gasped with the hatred that was stifling me, and caught myself thinking that even this spasmodic panting was an ideological repetition, an imitation of her asthmatic breathing. As the years went by, the hateful details of her image became ever more so, because I was recognizing them ever more clearly in myself. All that is good in us comes from God, all that is bad comes from our parents. I sighed in relief: her death had freed me from my self-hatred. Just as long as the reverse wasn't the case, when, with the death of the parent, the entire legacy of the character traits you detested, those mannerisms, that intonation, passes on into the sole custody of the offspring. The fateful lot of a surviving twin.

I tried to get into a melancholy mood with traditional thoughts along the lines of your mother being the only creature in the world who loves you without thought of reward: with her death, so my thoughts ran, ended the earthly ration of disinterested love in others towards you. All these sad reflections *à la* Yesenin on the subject of my old mother failed to help: the blessed tear did not start to my eyes nor did a lump appear in my throat; the throbbing persisted in my temples, which were now parchment-dry, like an old man's. The abnormality of my condition was shown by the total displacement of my ideas about the point and significance of the most commonplace actions. Every morning I would recall with equal concern that it was time to go to the kitchen and make some tea, and not to forget to commit suicide on the way back. I did neither the one nor the other. Towards the end of the day I used to fall into a state of total paralysis.

Once I stretched my arm out towards a cup of coffee on the table and half-way there realized that I hadn't the strength to reach it: I knew that even if I did reach it, it would be all the same as if I didn't. All of a sudden it became crystal clear, not simply that everything had ended—but that it was perfectly possible *there never had been anything anyway*. Time stood still. I feared to stir. The attitude of grief is the attitude of calm, because any movement can lead to being drawn into another life, whereas grief is solidarity with death. A living creature freezes motionless when it feigns death and pretends to be a corpse; waiting till dark before crawling out of the common grave after the massacre—or seizing the enemy's throat when he turns away from your carcass. I was pretending to be dead out of self disgust. The death of someone close is like a mirror. Your own life is correspondingly diminished—to that past made up of the things you held in common. The fact that I had not reacted at all to the death of my mother attested above all to my self-disgust. I wanted to find myself abroad—somewhere outside myself.

The villa was a stone's throw from the cliff, which led precipitously down to a vast deserted beach—the holiday season was over. The rhythmic ebb and flow of the tides was audible from the house at any time of the day or night, ceaselessly proclaiming the reassuring thought that life was going on without me. I'd be left in peace. In the mornings I would saunter along the edge of the sand as far as a rocky cove where the bay came to an end, and where the ocean used to leave a pile of jetsam on the pebbles like a sacrificial offering— Coca-Cola cans, old newspapers, a legless doll, watermelon rinds, everything the steamship passengers tossed overboard. Towards evening, incensed that even the seagulls were ignoring the refuse, the incoming tide would engulf it all again. Meanwhile, I would have spent the whole day staring at the off-white horizon under the awning of a surfing-hut, vacated after the summer, having lunched in a beach café on the inevitable grilled sea-perch, washed down, Portuguese fashion, not with white wine but red, and made my slow and pleasantly ponderous way back up the steps to the villa.

The villa itself was a rather neglected one-story house, the sort that's called a bungalow and not a hacienda, which had over the years accumulated an endless maze of little rooms, with verandas and inner courtyards, box-rooms and stairs up to the balustraded roof. The great virtue of the house lay in the fact that this jumble of apartments was so delightful that there was no need to go outside, apart from sunning oneself in the rocking chair of an afternoon out on the lawn, fanned by the sea breeze, with a glass of Portuguese wine in your hand and a pointless book on your knee. I would be far from sober by this hour of the day and, gazing at the treetops turning pink as the sun sank in the sky, I was inclined to turn sundry

philosophical conclusions and syllogisms over in my mind—
that year they revolved around a comparison between the
English eighteenth century gothic novel and the phenomenon
of the third wave of Russian emigration. This metaphysical
conundrum, pleasantly fuddled with alcohol, found an illustration in the never-ending arabesques which the semi-wild
cats would perform in front of me with the zeal of harem
women. These cats, who carried on a polygamous existence in
all the hutches and sheds of the house's enormous garden,
used to appear in the hope of finding something to their ad-
vantage every time I sat down in the chair. They created the
sense of contrast I needed—a balletic impression of perpetual
motion, convincing me that my condition of inner paralysis
was not an illusion.

The uninvited visitor appeared towards the evening of a thick,
sultry day. It wasn't the traditional seasonal heat of the Portuguese coast, it was a hazy heat presaging a thunderstorm.
Everything was still, creating an illusion of expectancy, which
in turn produced a feeling of being on edge. When the iron
gate clinked and she appeared at the end of the garden walk, I
thought that some prying little local girl had wandered into
the villa grounds out of curiosity. Her plaits, bound with silk
ribbon, at once caught my eye. She clacked along the stone
slabs in heavy leather sandals.

"What a marvelous garden you've made here—figs, if
I'm not mistaken? And ripe figs at that!" She began walking
round the garden, eyeing each edible fruit she encountered
with a predatory keenness. It was only now I noticed the old-
fashioned panama hat she was holding and the cheap hippy
necklace; its bony beads clattered as if to drown the creaking
of her rheumatic joints and the chirping of her bright little
voice.

"Pardon?" I recovered myself, asking her, English-fashion, to repeat the question she had not yet put in Russian.

"Serafima Bobrik-Donskaya," she bowed, bobbing at the knees. Her large button-like eyes stared unblinkingly, while her mouth seemed to open of its own accord, as if it were worked on strings, bringing her pendulous cheeks into play. Her face seemed ready to purse itself tearfully at any moment. Some very old ladies do have infant-school faces like that, especially when their plaits hang down at either side. Noticing the bewilderment in my expression, she started chattering away again. The gist was that she was Varvara von Lubeck's best friend and, chancing to be passing, had decided to look round the villa, as she was intending to spend the following summer here with her son and was looking out for a bigger house than she was renting at the moment, not far off, without her son, though it was the first summer holiday she had spent without him, incidentally, without her son, all on her own.

"I fixed myself up here in Abufera, quite near. Charming little *shpot!*" Since she was chewing on some figs she'd picked during all this, every "s" turned into a lisping "sh" sound.

Abufera (quite near, to be sure) was one of those frightful little holiday resorts which had sprung up in the last few years as a result of the tourist boom. Concrete high-rise buildings with balconies now dominated the little hill overlooking the fishermen's huts and the grimy nooks and crannies of the old center. "I found a wonderful little room in old Abufera. I breathe the scents of ancient Portugal. I enjoy myself on next to nothing, it's just incredibly cheap. You and I are English, so it's *à notre avantage:* the sterling exchange rate is incredibly high—strike while the sterling's hot, as the saying goes, do you travel much yourself?"

I didn't at once realize that I had been asked a question.

Naturally, I made no reply. That was her way: say something, some nonsense about herself, then shoot a question at you. It was a poorly-laid stratagem: nosing out my habits and preferences, relying on a reciprocal frankness on my part. The main thing was not to answer questions, not to allow myself to get involved in social intercourse, however innocent the question might seem at first glance. I watched her in silence with the sort of expression you have when you don't know whether your narrow-eyed grimace means you're trying to put on a benevolent face, or you're just incapable of concealing the hatred and exasperation tearing you apart inside. I sat in my chair without stirring, contemplating her large dragon-fly head in the panama hat, her thin legs in their masculine sandals, the unceremonious nature of her appearance; her manner, very common in émigré circles, was so out of place under this Atlantic sky, that it transformed her into a kind of apparition. It only wanted for me to sit out the whole evening with her in a spiritualist séance: this ghost of three emigrations from Russia was clearly looking forward to a heart-to-heart conversation with a fellow-countryman. The evening had been ruined; the walk along the Atlantic beach in the sunset, then later, in the rocking chair, lending half an ear to the tidings of distant disasters, one squinting eye drooping in a half-doze over a boring book. The evening had been destroyed, the night had been destroyed, and the next day; my hermit-like peace had been destroyed—everything, because I had to sit, listen, and nod assent to this incessant lisping, chattering, and twittering.

"Personally, I'm an inveterate traveller. I've emigrated three times. Where haven't I been over the years? I remember once in the Sinai desert the roof over my head was the shell of an abandoned motorcar. We were wakened by the crying of camels. All around, bloodthirsty Bedouins were waving their scimitars: apparently a rusting car chassis means as much in prestige to them as a brand new Rolls-Royce to a London *nouveau riche!* Did you come out through Israel by any chance?" Finding no response in my face, as stony as the tablets of Moses, she went on: "I'm at home everywhere. I'm an internationalist. As opposed to our English folk, I sense a kind of mystical kinship with everyone. Do you sense a mystical kinship with other peoples? When I'm sun-tanned, people in England take me for a Pakistani woman—that comes from my Ukrainian-Romanian blood. Talking of the East, incidentally, in Morocco, after the war, we refugees built an orthodox church. Wood is terribly hard to get hold of in Morocco—so we run about like little kids, one brings in a cardboard box, a lump of wood to tack on, or a beer crate. So then, the Moroccan lads there spoke to me in Moroccan, taking me for one of their own. With my Eastern European pronunciation, my *parlez-vous français* sounded just like Moroccan. You didn't get to know Varvara Von Lubeck at Father Blum's, did you?"

Another pause. She was unembarrassed.

"I find a common language with everybody. I got off the bus in Abufera and I was offered a room straightaway. The owner of the house said I looked like a Portuguese—otherwise he wouldn't have offered me the rent. I can easily make myself understood in Spanish, so I'm very familiar with the Portuguese roots. If it wasn't for their idiosyncratic accent, those 'sh' and 'zh' sounds—and still they say that 'zh' is exclusive to Russian, ha! But really, what a nice family they are. They do everything their own sweet way. Delightful room looking out on the sea. True, the other window has a view of the kitchen next door. Sometimes the owners sit up late in there, and you just can't sleep. On the other hand you save on the electricity—you don't need a table-lamp: just lie there and read in bed, it's as bright as day through the window. Of course I have to go in and out through the kitchen. But there's advantages in that too: you can always grab something—an olive, say, or a bit of fish. The fish here is wonderful. The Portuguese are a fishing people—do you like fish? My son and I always eat fish according to season. It's on the dear side in London, but it's dirt cheap here in Abufera. They don't let me use the stove, though, but there's a charming Portuguese on the beach and he grills grey mullet over a fire—or is it sardines? He sometimes lets me grill one or two fish on his fire. In Abufera, you know, all the quays have little tables and the fishermen, fascinating simple toilers of the sea, catch the sardines literally in the depths of the waves and fry them before your eyes. All hell breaks loose, everybody getting photographed. I don't really understand why they have to be photographed—what's so specially exotic about a fried sardine? No, you know, when you're a long way from home, the most commonplace things seem extraordinary. Would you like to regale yourself on fried fish? Just imagine, my son loves bony flatfish—he's absolutely mad about them! While I'm away, I expect he's found himself some really skinny wench."

She seemed not to be addressing me as she spoke that last sentence. As if at the mention of fish, the cats began circling round her: they had immediately recognized in her one of their own. She proffered them a partly-eaten fig. The cats rushed for her hand, necks outstretched, only to recoil in disappointment after one sniff. She, meanwhile, was gradually pushing me back into the house, advancing upon me as surely as if she had a knife in her hand, with her constant recitative and feline accompaniment. I was retreating into the kitchen. When she reached the threshold, she pointed somewhere above my shoulder to the shelf, where some china roosters from the Portuguese market were flaunting themselves.

"I keep looking at those things, I just can't take my eyes off them. That bright-colored rooster takes me right back to my beloved Ukrainian steppes or the Carpathian forests. You're flying, you know, like in Gogol, then comes the sound of a string plucking in the mist and you look down at the ground and, good gracious, but it's Portugal!" She began relating the legend of how the rooster became the national emblem of Portugal; about the holy pilgrim who was accused of stealing and was about to be burned at the stake, and how he beseeched God and God transformed the gnawed bones on the judge's dinner plate into a live crowing rooster. The hackneyed legend came straight from the pages of some dog-eared guidebook.

"I read about the rooster in my guidebook—it's an astonishing bible of facts, published by a most respectable firm, it's where my son works. It is our wont to read aloud to one another, I have to do most of the reading—well I'm the mother, when all's said and done! You like reading aloud to one another? My son works as a translator in this very respectable translation firm, translating into foreign languages, never stopping. But we always have breakfast and supper to ourselves. We pour out our hearts to each other; talking away, we forget there's a world outside. You see, they're the only times when we can talk to our heart's content. Though I'm the one who does most of the talking, old chatterbox that I am."

I pictured the son to myself, coming home and sitting down to table on a squeaky chair. Suspenders, patches of sweat under the arms. Sunset on a hot day, the clock ticking, the radio on low.

"But what about something to get the teeth round? It's all these bus changes, I'm just talking my head off: not so much as a crumb has passed my lips, not a bite since brekker." As she talked, little snatches of slang kept surfacing unexpectedly, picked up no doubt on the railway platforms, trains, and in the station buffets of her three emigrations, a mixture of countries, decades, and generations. She was looking at me expectantly with those wide bulging eyes, which made her face look tiny. She was certain I would offer her supper. That was all I needed. We would sit as the sun went down on a stifling day. The chairs would creak slightly. The clock tick. The radio be on low. She would fill up the ringing vacancy in my temples with her ceaseless émigré gossip and gibberish about the past, present, and future of Russia.

Through the refrigerator door, which seemed just to have become transparent, I could see the piece of smoked ham I had been intending to fry up with some eggs for my supper—with a bottle of harsh, heavy rioja, not to mention the tin of octopus and a glass of medronia, a kind of Portuguese grappa. I licked my lips. It was then I noticed her wind-reddened eyes and mouth half open in expectation. She loudly gulped down her saliva.

"Let me organize something lovely and tasty for you. The Warsaw dissidents thought a lot of my lazy curd dumplings, as I remember. Do you have any cottage cheese?" She reached out for the refrigerator and the door opened part way as if magnetized, but I flung myself at it like a hero of the fatherland covering a machine-gun barrel with his chest, and slammed it shut. I mumbled something incoherent about not cooking here, just eating in the local restaurants, but today I'd had a late lunch and didn't intend to have supper at all, so don't judge me too severely and so on and so forth.

"Oh, don't bother yourself," she said unexpectedly, though I hadn't moved a finger. She'd understood, apparently. "I'll drop round to the café; I noticed a charming little glass-sided place just a minute away. Won't you accompany me? Appetite grows with the eating, *mon cher*. If you change your mind, you're welcome to join me in the beach institution," she said with the playful manner of the society lioness, and swinging her traveling-bag coquettishly, made her way along the stone slabs to the gate, masculine sandals clacking as she went. In those sandals, her thin bare legs reminded me of nettles growing through stout collective farm fences.

As soon as the latch on the cast-iron gate clicked behind her, I raced to the phone to ring the owner of the house in London. Varvara von Lubeck had difficulty in recalling Serafima Bobrik-Donskaya. According to her, they could only have met once at an Orthodox charity tea at Pushkin House. "She's a scrounger, that Serafima. And her son's an oaf, tied to his mummy's apron strings. I never promised her anything. Throw her out neck and crop," said the old woman, and concluded by swearing with aristocratic refinement.

I felt I had just got rid of some hateful school exam and drank off a large glass of burning medronia. I felt famished. I cut off a huge slice of smoked ham and began tearing at it impatiently with my teeth, swallowing down the partly-chewed pieces, afraid she would be back any minute. After the conversation with von Lubeck, I was half looking forward to her return—a confrontation with this unceremonious parasite. When I had exposed her lies about her relationship with von Lubeck, I would have an excuse for saying: I'm sorry, but in the circumstances I can see no possibility of carrying on our conversation. I pictured myself getting to my feet, leaning my hand on the chair-back, insolently hanging over the table in a half-bow, saying: "In view of everything that has been said, I consider it impossible to continue our conversation," then adding something brief and polite, chillingly neutral. In the light of my imminent release from this tiresome uninvited guest, and the growing conviction of being in the right about recovering my hard-earned freedom, my temples were buzzing joyfully. Apparently my feeling of depression was passing off—as usual, because of an incomprehensible and half-accidental chain of trivial events, restoring self-confidence and hope for the future. I walked out onto the asphalt path leading to the beach to spy out the land: what could my visitant be doing in the dark?

The modernist glass cube of the establishment on the shore was neon-lit from inside, seeming to accelerate the onset of darkness all around. It was deserted in there. The bored waitress informed me that the lady had not ordered anything. She had simply wrapped up in her napkin the things which are put out with the knives and forks according to the rather odd Portuguese custom; self-opening tins of fish, butter in a little plastic container, and a dryish bread-roll—something like a tourist's breakfast, or a bite to eat when three tramps split a bottle. Actually, one was supposed to pay for these odds and ends as well, but the waitress had assumed that the lady vagabond was my guest and set down the loss to my account. The old Russian stinginess when traveling: always at someone else's expense, never staying in hotels, always with some friend or relative up to, and including, slight acquaintances of forgotten slight acquaintances. That went for food too; they either carried it with them, tucked away half-rotten from home, or half-stolen, pocketed for nothing as occasion offered.

Out of doors the wind was rising and the sky was beginning to fill with nocturnal clouds in the last rays of the sun. The lonely light on the parapet in front of the café, reflected off the whitecaps, invited one to jump, before it was too late, onto that improvised luminous ladder leading to the horizon. That was where the clouds were coming from: they would halt, snagged on the mountain peaks, then move backwards, as if having second thoughts about emigrating. A fishing-smack, or schooner or felucca—God knows what sort of vessel it was—lay half a mile off shore. It was only an old rusted hulk, beached on the shoal many years before. In the evening light, the skeletal wreck looked like some romantic Flying Dutchman. I was moving along the edge of the cliff above the beach, searching for my ill-starred impostor in the thickening twilight. By now I was really angry with her, not only for disturbing my own funereal vigil, but for making me worried over her disappearance. At length I caught sight of her panama hat on the rocks of the cove where the tide used to deposit the detritus of civilization. Serafima Bobrik-Donskaya had obviously not seen all the Coca-Cola tins and ripped polythene bags—or had haughtily ignored them and seated herself in front of the incoming tide, rolling up her skirt as she carelessly dangled her sandals in the sea. She was chewing on her roll, holding her panama on with one hand as the wind got up.

After a while, she got down from the rock and, picking her way carefully, approached the tide-line as if it were a caged beast. With an access of lyrical sadness totally absurd at such an hour in such weather, she had started to break off bits of bread and throw them into the ocean. Who was she feeding? The seagulls? The sharks? The clouds, perhaps. The more she swung her arm, hurling the fragments of bread, the thicker grew those night clouds, shrouding the inky sky. She took her shoes off and sat down on the pebbles by the very edge of the surf. I couldn't make anything out in the darkness, apart from her white panama. Then came the sound of her singing borne on the wind. At first, I imagined the voice was coming from the café, or one of the villas on the shore had started playing an old cracked record. The harsh "r", the "kh" sound and the hard "i" in among the sibilants sometimes combine to produce a phonetic resemblance between Russian and Portuguese. But phonetics apart, I now began to make out the words too. The words were Russian—"But our years are flying, our years like black birds are flying"—she was howling out the long-drawn phrases in the manner of Claudia Shulzhenko, the Russian Vera Lynn. At social gatherings, I sometimes liked to come out with my (at first sight) paradoxical notion, that we émigrés had to get used to the idea of lacking a single past and realize that there were many pasts. However, her nostalgic excursions into émigré folklore from Siberia to Morocco had irritated me by their incoherence, although she herself felt no sense of split personality. *But the years are flying, our years like black birds are flying.* A pause ensued. She had faltered. Either she'd run out of breath, or she'd forgotten the words, or the words had been carried out to sea by a gust of wind. *And they have no time to look back.* This *ba-a-ack* sounded hoarse, cracked and unnatural. I was convinced that it was no longer singing I heard, but rather a suppressed weeping, almost a groan.

I went back to the villa and started putting the lights on. In the maze of rooms which had accumulated over the years, a child's construction of cardboard houses, there were recesses, corners, doorways at every step in a chaotic agglomeration, like reflections in a shattered mirror. In every niche, every nook and cranny, there was the inevitable lamp. Standard lamps, night-lights, electric candelabras, and ordinary naked electric lights lit up the enfilading rooms with positively theatrical inventiveness. Whether the owner of the villa conceived of life as a series of mysterious theatrical stages or was simply mortally afraid of the dark, the effect was that, in the evenings, the house used to shine out like a huge lampshade. My visitor appeared like a moth to the flame.

"You should have joined in my riotous living, young man. They're so marvellously romantic, these Portuguese! They sang me some lovely romances to the guitar, the fado—they remind me so much of our gypsies. I had some wonderful fish assorti with cockles and mussels and all kinds of meat. Then I sat by the shore of the ocean, admiring the moonlight scenery. Marvellous reflexes on the water!"

"Reflexes?"

"Well, you know, the mirror reflections made by the moon. Marvellous reflexes!"

I winced. She'd dragged in the moon as a bit of phoney romance—I'd seen it with my own eyes: there was no moon, the sky was completely clouded over. That émigré habit of telling lies and being in ecstasy over everything, to justify the cost of the trip, so to speak; after all, if we've sunk so much effort into getting here, everything must be ideal once we've arrived—or at least appear so. That must be the logic of optimists in general; the secret fear that their efforts in living should turn out not to be justified. Breakfast on the grass turns into a dry roll and fish on bare rock in the darkness.

"You know, I'm a traveling frog, but to me personally the exotic means nothing. Here in my breast," and she placed her little clenched fist on her chest in the Spanish communard gesture, "here in my breast lie African jungles. When finances are low, I can even be sitting in London and Portugal is in my heart. The thing is to train the imagination. I'll make a little marmite sandwich—you like marmite? My son and I adore English marmite, lovely and salty, then off on the steamer down the Thames to Greenwich. We have such jolly lunches together sometimes. We sit down under a bush with a view of the Cutty Sark—there's your jungle for you. Give me a marmite sandwich and a decent novel under a bush in Greenwich and Portugal means nothing! I've emigrated three times and I can tell you one thing, nobody wants a bore or a whiner. I always try to look on the bright side of life. You know, forget the hurts. And the wrongs. That's the way my tiny mind works anyway. I'm very lucky in that sense. I'm really a very lucky little soul. I'm all for auto-suggestion. You feel what you think. I always tell myself: everything's all right, no need to get the wind up or start crying your eyes out. You have to fire other people with your own example, not just sit and mope.

Depression does pass off, you know. 'I trust again, shed tears again, and such relief, relief . . .' as the poet said at a difficult time in his life. I want to dance all night, like Eliza Doolittle sings in the famous musical. Are you interested in the theatrical arts?"

Talking of theatrical arts, this was the most suitable moment to expose her fibbing. It was now or never.

"Varvara von Lubeck rang, the owner of this house, I mean," I began, coughing and faltering. Resting my hand on the chair-back, I went on with affected carelessness, gazing arrogantly across her at the garish roosters: "Varvara von Lubeck, by the way, knows nothing about your intention of renting this villa. Varvara von Lubeck hardly remembers you at all in fact." I heaved a profound sigh. Now was the time to say: "In view of which . . ."

"But I never had any such intention," said my visitor, not a whit discomfited; her voice was unexpectedly husky. Her face grew thinner and more pinched. "Until I'd seen the house, I had no intentions at all. I just felt I needed to see a familiar face, that's why I trudged over here from Abufera. As for renting, that notion occurred to me later. My experience in emigration has taught me to leave everything to the last possible moment. The chief thing in our existence is to make no plans and rely on nothing, so you don't get disappointed afterwards. However, my memory erases everything bad. Probably because it's so hard for the heart to bear pain and unpleasantness. At least for my little heart it is. It's just a little thing and often goes beating away, beating away. Pulpitation. Do you suffer from pulpitation?"

These blatantly sentimental Chekhovian *pulpitations* were the last straw for me. It was emotional blackmail. How long is it going to be before we Russians squeeze the last drop of Chekhov from our veins? "You know, my little heart goes pit-a-pat to the sound of the incoming tide. The sound of the tide, the smell of grass, the whiteness of cumulus clouds—they're all different in different countries, but it's the same nevertheless: they remind you of the tide, the grass and the clouds of your homeland. I get positively drunk with nostalgia, when I hear the sound of the surf, then I looked at my watch—good heavens, all the buses will have stopped running! So much for planning the future . . ."

I knew it would end up like this. She supposedly didn't know the buses in Portugal stopped running so early: the Spanish culture after all was one of siestas and carnival nights. They sleep during the day and ride the buses from the carnival to the dance-hall. Still, in an enormous hacienda like this ("bungalow, not hacienda," I corrected her), there must surely be some corner, cubby-hole, or asylum? For just one night? She had emigrated three times and was used to the minimum of amenities. She could perhaps snuggle down on the sofa over there in the corner, or on the rugs here. She recalled the coach-loads of refugees traveling from occupied Paris to Marakech, to the tune of a gramophone record from *Casablanca*. And before that, as a charwoman alongside her interned husband: a besom broom under her head now and again, or an overturned filing-cabinet. She could use that Scottish plaid as a blanket perfectly well or there, that old coat. She slept like a mouse. She only needed a few hours sleep, like Stalin (that's a joke, she giggled). Come the dawn, there'd be no sign of her. She looked piteously at me with her washed-out button eyes.

I left her alone with the refrigerator to finish off her tea without me—my resistance had been utterly broken. She drank country-fashion, out of the saucer, hunching herself up like an old woman and blowing on it, as if to drive away the evil influences clinging to the edges. I heard her clacking off in her leather sandals into one of the little rooms—"I'll sit by myself and thumb through my little dictionary to learn some new Portuguese words. With my knowledge of Spanish, it'll be like Ukrainian to a Russian. A new language will come in handy in the future." If she behaved like a mouse, it was a truly indefatigable rodent. I tossed and turned, listening to the constant rustling, knocking, and clanking from the other end of the house. Apparently she had decided to wash the dishes in the kitchen, attempting to do me a good turn, or else she'd started sorting out the things in her traveling-bag, throwing the stuff around the floor: or perhaps she'd decided to tidy the house up and was crashing the furniture about, or she was simply wandering through the rooms out of curiosity, assuming I was sound asleep.

I couldn't really get to sleep. Half-dozing, half-delirious, I lay between two zones—whether inside me or outside, it would be hard to say. I had to freeze into stillness, not budging, not a single muscle quivering, not a single hair stirring: otherwise I would slip into the other zone where all my innards were in uproar, where everything twitched and leapt, jostled and scratched. I wasn't sure what it was, but I knew for certain that it only needed the least error, for me to allow myself the slightest false step and my state of eternal peace would be shattered at once and I would slit her down and in, and there would be no escape from incessant fighting, struggle, conflict, head-achingly wearisome with its endless balletic repetition. I hunched up, so as not to slip down into that naked and shuddering chaos. It began to shrivel before my eyes and localize, finally, into my stomach. I couldn't relax the muscles around my navel for a second. There inside, thrashing and scratching, hammering its fists and jerking every limb was something bearing the name of Serafima Bobrik-Donskaya. She was trying to tear her way through to the outside world, to fight free of me and my fleshly envelope.

When I finally emerged from that half-doze, half-delirium,

it dawned on me that I was suffering fearful gripes in the stomach. I'd probably got food-poisoning—or, no, it was the result of my greedy haste in demolishing the smoked ham, gulping it down unchewed while my uninvited guest was strolling about on the beach. The pain was nauseating, as if threads were being pulled inside my stomach. I started to squeal from the spasms of colic, then clenched my teeth, plunging my face into the pillow. Then at once, almost like an echo, came the half-singing, half-howling of my midnight somnambulist from the other end of the house. At any rate, that was what it seemed like to me as I passed from my bedroom into the hall: that was the way mad people crooned to themselves, those atonal trillings and senseless intonational leaps without beginning or end, so quiet and careful, seeming to compose what to them appears to be a complex and beautiful melody. Suddenly, a spurt of water from above squirted into my face. It was as if somebody standing on the roof was relieving himself, perhaps trying to bring me to my senses.

And all at once, the source of the maniacal sounds, the rustlings, and the knockings, was revealed. The huge, squat house was being rocked by the squalling wind. The draft was whistling and howling through the endless alcoves, corridors, and crannies of the house, as if it were trying to soothe an aching tooth by pacing back and forth. In an unexpected gesture of irritation, an unsteady home-made standard lamp was overturned, and to the flash of the bursting filament was added that of the lightning outside the window. In the middle of the hall stood Serafima. Her bare flaccid-skinned elbows stuck out of the sleeves of a shoddy nightgown. She had loosened her plaits before going to bed, and the tufts sticking up behind her balding pate gave her the look of a crazy university professor. The shock of the thunder shook the windowpanes, through which the fig trees were lit up as they bent before the blast, surrounded by a hail of falling fruit. The shuddering windows found an echo in yet another shower of water from under the roof. From the next angle came an answering gurgling trill.

The squat, sturdy house had been the embodiment of coziness, of a slightly eccentric and somewhat absurd kind, somehow trusting in its architectural insouciance and confident that the forces of nature would treat it kindly. It had seemed to raise its hat in greeting to the lowering heavens as the foul weather came on—and the roof indeed turned out to be as full of holes as an old panama.

Serafima Bobrik-Donskaya stood in the middle of the hall, with a luminous socialist-realist smile on her face, stretching her hands aloft to catch the streaming rain, just like the heroine of a Stalinist film about the spring of socialism. I thought the thunder, the lightning, and the whole horror of earthly existence had finally driven her off her head. I rushed into the kitchen to get jugs, bowls, and cloths to stem the flood. My uninvited guest meanwhile had rolled up her sleeves and set to work. She was taking up the carpets and moving the sofas and chairs out of the way, squeezing out the cloths, and emptying the constantly filling bowls and buckets. Her face shone with inspiration. Now I understood why: the hour of trial had arrived, when it was clear that I couldn't cope by myself. Her self-confidence grew with every passing moment. Unlike me, she knew what to do. Bucket and cloth in hand, she took charge. Her back is etched on my memory: she was kneeling down and wiping up a huge pool of rain water on the floor and wringing out the cloth over a bucket. Up and down went her elbows, tufts of hair clung to her scalp and a rivulet of sweat ran down her bare neck. Getting up yet again to empty an overflowing bucket, she surveyed me with the triumphant gleam of one proved right: she had demonstrated that her arrival at the house had not been in vain.

"I can't see any end to this rain, and that applies to her

staying here. I can't very well throw her out tomorrow morning in weather like this, can I?" I reflected glumly as I listened to the sound of the cloudburst and the asthmatic wheeze of her breathing.

She seemed to divine the secret thought in my face and gasped as she clutched at her heart. Her knees buckled and she began to sink down and sag to one side. I seized her round the waist and like some ludicrous ballroom couple (up till now I had been afraid of touching her) led her over to a couch. She started and blinked at the lightning flashes beyond the window, which brazenly caught us embracing like clandestine lovers among the debris of what had so recently been domestic comfort, between the pools of rain water rippling in the wind. The walls seemed to have disappeared: we were standing on the stage sets of an Atlantic beach.

This time, however, she was clearly in no mood for cheap dramatic effects: her face began to take on a floury hue, whitening outwards from the nose. An asthmatic whistle broke through her wrinkled, half-open mouth. The ghostly smile had not left her lips, as if it were agonizingly difficult for her to alter her facial expression. She had obviously had a heart attack, pre-infarction condition or something of the kind, clearly something to do with the heart anyway. I started to panic and rushed over to the phone, but there was little point, in weather like this and at this hour, in a one-horse town where a Chekhovian doctor had nothing to do except put away the medronia and masticate smoked ham.

To get to the medical center in the town from our villa on the shore, you had to cross a small valley, a sort of gully. Stunted olives grew along the verges of the stony road, swimming in silver thickets, and preserving the calm of biblical camels amid the swirling wind and lashing rain, terrifying thunderclaps and occasional street-lamps. Their light rocked upwards like a fishing-float in the torrents of water. All along the road in the surrounding murk flickered mysterious glimmerings: only when I heard a chance half-squeal, half-miaow over by the fencing did I realize that these were stray cats under the shed awnings observing my progress like an escort ready to raise the alarm at the slightest hint of moral weakness or any attempt at deviation from the appointed goal. Although the road went almost straight up a hill, I wasn't conscious of my burden at first; she seemed to weigh less in my arms than her flowered nightgown. I tried to remember some local equivalent for the word "validol" (valicordin? valium?), but she was preventing me from concentrating by going on with her asthmatic widow's twittering, perhaps trying to deaden the sound of the heavenly washing machine or perhaps the beating of her disordered heart.

"I rent a room on the hill. It's hard getting back up there with my asthma. But in the mornings it's really lovely running down the tunnels to the sea. You know the famous caves there, tunnels hollowed out by the mountain streams. Spring torrents. The streams have all dried up but the tunnels are still there. In the morning, because of them you can be in the sea naked in seconds. Nudism isn't against the law here, you know?" I pictured her running down naked into the sea. Tufts of hair on her head bouncing. Flesh flopping. "But I allow myself that luxury, because this time I'm on holiday without my son."

She bit her lip and gasped. Suddenly she gripped my arm convulsively and whispered in violation of all the barriers of intimacy between us: "Well, what a swine, eh? Abandon a mother on the road, can you imagine?" I didn't know who she was talking to. To nobody, seemingly. But in my alarm I took everything she said to apply to me.

She had suddenly become terribly heavy. My left shoulder was aching and I had to halt under the next olive tree to shift her onto the other arm, like an awkward suitcase. Under a lamp, I saw a crimson stain of blood seeping through the nightgown on her chest. Or was it just an effect of the light? In a panic, I fell to my knees and started unbuttoning the nightgown, trying to think what I could use as a bandage . . . and then encountered a hard lump by the breast pocket. She was gazing past me; her button eyes were squinting as if they had been sewn on in the wrong place. The breast pocket proved to contain an unripe fig, whose juicy crimson pulp, when crushed, had spread into a bloody patch.

"That's what he said: I'm fed up with you, mother. I'm leaving you to your fate. Find somebody else to torment with your three emigrations! He left me with nothing but a handbag at the airport. He took most of the money, left me with the bare minimum and a return ticket in two weeks. In a foreign country. So I'm an expatriate again? My pockets are full of pills," she mumbled tearfully. "I've got pulpitations. I'm all alone. Nobody needs me in the whole world. Where do I go to now? Emigrate another three times? When I was the resident of a totalitarian regime at one time and dreamed of escape to freedom, I pictured such an extraordinary, inimitable world of light and ecstasy. I so wanted everything in my life to be extraordinary—even death. I fled from a grave—common, like everything else under communism, yes. But now, with you, I feel drawn to that idea—it's dawned on me: you can start your life all over again from the beginning without crying your eyes out, can't you? I've got masses of free time now, and I'm an absolutely independent creature. I could get work as a cook, you know, I'm a real culinary specialist. I can make a marvellous goulash, one of my husbands was a Hungarian, you know that? Once it was Gulag, now it's goulash."

A grimace distorted her face and it was hard to tell whether it was a lopsided ironic smile, a convulsive sob, or a stab of pain from her heart. I suggested she keep quiet for a while and make it easier for herself. But she wouldn't subside.

"How can it be that I speak practically every language on earth and at the end of my life I am left without a single person to talk to me?"

Again she became lighter and lighter in my arms. Gradually she lapsed into complete silence, her face like one asleep. I was terrified I might not get her to the hospital alive. I plunged on and on along that unseen track into the geography of that unfamiliar valley through a landscape set on end by the hurricane: the rain was lashing my face, just as it had done when my mother had dragged me to the collective farm hospital half a dozen miles from home. She had carried me on her back along a washed-out farm track through the sucking mud, wheezing asthmatically, or perhaps because I was clinging tight round her neck in fear, pain, and shame.

I remember the hair matted on the back of her skull and the stream of rain running down the back of her head and into the neck of her dress. It was hard going for her: I was about six years old then, and I was a sturdy lad. That was in the settlement near Moscow where my granddad used to work as head doctor. Some friends and I had climbed into the collective farm garden the night before and stolen a sackful of apples. The apples were small and hard—about the size of figs, green and unripe: they really set our teeth on edge, but we doggedly went on munching them, competing with one another. Because they were free, we stuffed ourselves; they were something God-given, and so we couldn't reject them. Towards evening I developed colicky pains and by midnight I was writhing in agony. Half-dozing, half-delirious, it seemed I had to freeze into stillness and not move a single muscle, because any movement would give me away and I would never get over the garden fence. The fever was just a result of stomach ache, but mother was certain it was appendicitis. I was afraid to tell her that it would get better by itself. She would have known then that I knew what had caused the pain and I would have to confess about the stolen apples. I preferred to keep quiet. She decided to carry me to hospital as a matter of urgency. I was afraid of the hospital, but I was even more afraid of confessing about the apples. I was a Soviet pioneer and didn't want to be thought a thief. I went on pretending I had appendicitis. The way to the hospital was along a farm track, washed out by heavy rain. I couldn't go by myself because of the colic. Mother strode out into the pitch dark through the clinging mud, bent under the weight of my body. She had panted, she sounded as if she was getting an attack of asthma.

"I see the light," my visitant's voice reached me.

"Light?" I asked. I had obviously taken her words in too lofty a spirit. What light could there be in such murk? "No, no, I see light breaking through the clouds. It's going to stop raining soon, and the night sky will be clear. I'll be able to get the bus to Abufera."

1990

Translated by Alan Myers

A CHANCE ENCOUNTER

I HAD ALREADY NOTICED HER AT ROGOZHSKY CEMETERY while I was standing by my mother's grave. The early light snow of a messy and impudent Russian winter had hurriedly powdered, as if for decency's sake, the dirty slush of the ground at my arrival, which made everything seem lighter. The bared trees still blocked the view along the pathways, but, as if ashamed of their ragged nakedness, they were ready at any moment to part and disperse, swayed and rocked by the wind. At first I paid no attention to the other figure in mourning vigil by the fence of the neighboring grave, some twenty paces from me: the stinging snow whipping from all directions turned this woman in the long coat among the naked trees into a scratched, blurred daguerrotype of the last century, so old-fashioned and dreamlike that memory instantly discarded it as irrelevant.

This momentary visual leap into another century, however, made my eye focus again hastily on the dates on my mother's gravestone, to convince myself that I could still tell the present from the past. This meeting with the past discouraged and befuddled my mind with a confused arithmetic. I had left thirteen years ago when I was thirty, that is, as old as my mother was when she gave birth to me. I mechanically calculated that I was now as old as she had been when she divorced my father. But to compare your age with your parents', as everyone knows, is pointless: when you get to be as old as they once were, they have reached a new, unattainable age, and so even at their "past" ages you seem younger to yourself than they looked at their time in your eyes.

This chase ends only at the finish line, when their whole life becomes part of your past. From the émigré, the "posthumous" point of view, time in abandoned Moscow also stops: for me, my mother would forever remain the same as when I had seen her for the last time on the day of my departure. After so many years of emigration I was allowed into Russia in order to see her grave: by her death my mother worked that feat at the Soviet border. They admit us to the past—as through Soviet customs and passport control—only at the expense of something lost in the present. Even a moment of recollection is a brief stop in time; the last stop, death, is a unity with the past. A return to the homeland.

I had tears in my eyes, as befits someone in a cemetery, but rather from the burning wind and snow salt than from grief, and, scornfully turning away from the slap of the wind, I hid my face in my raised collar and glanced to one side. These squalls of wind and snow were a good excuse not to look at the gravestone. The woman at the next grave remained motionless, as if waiting for me to leave. But I noticed her again on the way to the metro at the crossing where a crowd of drunkards swayed in the piercing wind at the beer stand, waiting for it to open, their faces distorted by the uniquely bestial look of hangover. She huddled at the side of the road, and I caught myself worrying that she would be spattered from head to toe by the November nostalgic slush, mud mixed with snow, from the wheels of the monsters on the road wafting gasoline and curses.

In the metro I didn't notice her on the platform—perhaps because of the crush, and then I forgot about her completely, stupefied by the image of Stalinism frozen in the marble and bronze of the interior. Time stopped, caught in a trap of carved doors with bronze handles and nickle-plated barriers. Museum instructions gazed down on the shoving visitors: stand on the right, pass on the left; it is forbidden to run on the escalators; give up your seat to passengers with children, the elderly, and invalids. I felt myself an invalid, I was an elderly child: an ageing person returns to his youth, to a country frozen in time. Give up your seats to elderly children, invalids of émigré time. The woodenness of these bureaucratic instructions took me back to the past most quickly of all. The encrusted interior of the subway cars, this calico relief of nauseating colors, separated me more firmly than any iron curtain from my London present. Mind the doors. Keep away from the edge of the platform. The next stop is emigration.

For an instant the car emptied, since some passengers had already got out and others had not yet crowded onto the train. At that moment I saw her again: she was sitting across from me, hunched up, her head drawn into her shoulders, leaning her cheek into her collar as if hiding her face. Suddenly she glanced right into my eyes and an ironic, I thought, barely noticeable smile hovered on her lips. It was quite possible that she was smiling to herself at some image flickering beyond the black underground glass where the lights of the tunnel flashed—a dark world existing in parallel with that present life to which there was no entrance for ordinary mortals. I remembered again where I had come from. The throng again crowded into the car and the woman disappeared. I got out at Prospect Marx.

The weather might have been specially designed to remove any desire for nostalgia—precisely because I had left the country in just this weather: an icy raw wind with sleet. On the eve of this October revolution Moscow has lost its last holiday decorations, party slogans, and posters, like some robbed widow. No fatherly smiles of the members of the Politburo or gleaming heroes of Socialist Labor. Only the humble banner "Happy Holiday" flapped in the wind, and the holiday atmosphere was so muted that at the end of the slogan there seemed to be not an exclamation mark but instead a question: "Happy Holiday?"

The streets, ragged to the point of nakedness, tried unsuccessfully to cover themselves with snow, these sparse wet November flakes which melted in motion and got in your eyes, ears, under your collar, like the fluff from a pillow torn open by a rapist. But I was shivering with joy from a vicious, almost perverse readiness to merge with this city again. I wanted this dark world that I had met anew to embrace me with its iron grip, cram me like a hat into the sleeve of the stone coat of the town. Instead, my native Moscow was emerging in front of my eyes like a childhood toy that had been stolen from my parents' house, and now it was impossible to prove, even to yourself, that it had been yours, so mauled had it been by someone else's hands. Like returning to your divorced wife: you remember everything, know everything down to the tiniest detail—the birthmark on the back, the curliness coming out of the underpants, and that she drinks coffee without sugar; but this woman is no longer yours, you no longer have the right to admit to yourself and others that you know everything about her.

"Keep four meters from the façade of the building," read the warning on the wall of my former house on Pushkin Street. What looked like a spiderweb of repair scaffolding were actually wooden shields: they hung over the sidewalks, protecting passers-by from decaying balconies and crumbling wall masonry. Under this heavy make-up it was impossible to discern the familiar contours of the window niches and portals. Diving under the archway into the courtyard I skirted some garbage bins and an iron door with yet another threatening exhortation, "Don't touch: high voltage"; I looked around the familiar place and found my window in the prison row of the fourth floor of the dirty-yellow wall. Ignoring both warnings to keep a safe distance, I strode into the enormous

entryway. A Soviet version of Proustian nostalgia, carried by
the urine and garbage underfoot, was illuminated by a naked
spattered bulb as dim as ageing memory. But I was happy:
such squalidness was absolutely inimitable. I flew up the
stairs. On the first landing a policeman barred my way. A
wooden barrier blocked the path upstairs to my apartment.
"What going on here?" I muttered in confusion. "Nothing's
going on here. This is the administration. Little Stage of the
Children's Theater. You should read the signs. Show your
pass." I had forgotten that the usual tenants had long since
been moved out and the building transferred to one of the
state institutions. To the Children's Theater. The division of
elder childhood, younger dotage?

For the first time during the week I'd been in Moscow, my
friends and relations had let me go for a walk on my own, as if
in reward for exemplary behavior, and then only with the
pardonable pretext that I wanted to spend time at my
mother's grave in solitude. And right away someone asks me
to show my pass, which didn't help me rid myself of the
general feeling of being a helpless infant lost in my own courtyard. I knew every corner and doorway of every building in
this town, but precisely this familiarity was making me feel
panicky: I remembered too much connected with this place
but was unable to recall a single concrete detail. It was like
reading forgotten pages of an old diary: you recognize the
words, even remember some of the circumstances connected
with the origins of these words. But the overall meaning of
these words, fragmented phrases, squiggles, is indecipherable.
Someone's highly illegible handwriting, resembling a . . .
but please, this is . . . almost, just a second, I know exactly
. . . And so on, but it never adds up to anything meaningful. . . .

I was nauseated from hunger. Between the National and
the Intourist—a striking juxtaposition, the names of these two

central hotels, straight out of the celebrated argument between the Slavophiles and the Westernizers—stood a wheeled stand with an absurdly summery awning and a few ridiculous little white resort tables, looking out of season in the wet snow. The inappropriateness of this moveable stand was increased by the sign *Bif-Grill* (by analogy with the Russian *bifstakes*, apparently), adding yet another wrongly-spelled freakish anglicism to the already overgrown third world of barbarisms in the empire of the Russian language. The Papuans of this third world sitting at the white tables looked like cephalopodic ricket victims, huge-headed from their gigantic fur hats and with earmuffs. It really is a third world: not heaven, not hell, but some third alternative—outside time and space: limbo. In the semi-darkness, beneath the snowflakes, as if considering some unresolvable question, they silently chewed some trash or other, contemplating the parallel darkness in which constantly humming and therefore seemingly soundless crowds of big-headed workers swam past in eddies of sidewalk crushes towards the entrance of the Prospect Marx metro stop. In that hum, some aphoristic pronouncements could be heard in repetitions, like "But in essence nothing has changed", or "Well, why always theirs?", and "But we also have . . ."

Enthralled, I approached the lit-up window of the stand. A girl with the bloody lips of a vampire in a white hospital smock leaned out and asked, as if it were a password: "*Bif-grill?*" And I repeated with the readiness of a conspirator: "*Bif-grill.*" Between two pieces of sticky grey sour-smelling bread, looking squashed, were two stinking meatballs, abundantly smeared with tomato paste. A paper cup of icy Pepsi-Cola was thrust into my other hand, although my teeth were chattering from the cold. I sniffed the *bif-grill* in my hand and, despite the itching despair in my stomach, went up to the dustbin and threw this culinary delicacy into it. And promptly caught the censuring glance of a half-starved person from behind me in the line. At least that's what I thought: having squeamishly thrown food away, I, the child of the famished postwar generation, silently condemned myself on the spot. But the glance from the line turned out not to be censuring at all: from a distance a loving glance can easily be confused with the stare of a prison warder.

"Zinovy! You are Zinovy?" Her formal "you" in addressing me was a token of politeness, marking the distance in years between our meetings; but there was also in this "you" something frivolous, almost obscene—it was the way a servant girl would coquettishly address the master when he stole up to her in the corridor. Apparently not only had she been looking at me on the sly, but I too had absent-mindedly been glancing at her, instinctively trying to confirm the feeling that the face was familiar.

On the trip from the cemetery to this eating place she had somehow managed to shorten the time gap between our meetings. Where had I seen these deep-set, pale grey eyes? These thin lips and strong chin? This short ash-tinted hairdo under a beret? From the cold she thrust her hands into the pockets of her garment that looked like a long old-fashioned greatcoat— and in this gesture, this pose, there was at once the defiance of a street urchin and an officer's sternness.

"You don't remember me, of course," she changed her tone to scepticism and irony, biting her lip and scowling. But when I, waving the tails of my green scarf, rushed towards her and kissed her cheek, her face immediately wrinkled touchingly in the sweet, familiar grimace of a sentimental smile: "Eugenia? Zhenia? Remember now? And I, just imagine . . ." But I anticipated and interrupted her with social deftness: "Of course, Eugenia, Zhenia, after so many a summer . . ." and she, of course, in an ironic echo, as if shooing away the flakes of wet snow, repeated: "So many a summer!"

134

I huddled and shuffled guiltily before her, like a good friend of bygone years who has forgotten his former girlfriend's birthday. Actually, I had absolutely no idea where and under what circumstances we used to see each other. All I could do was nod my head ingratiatingly, agree with any suggestion, and spread my arms in a gesture of commiseration while she recalled the names of our mutual friends who had left for the West or disappeared without a trace in the desert of Moscow's suburbia. She kept on mentioning anniversary celebrations and farewell parties, major dates of noisy gatherings, the impromptu rooms of our past carousals and the former crossings of our common routes. All this in some distorted light floated up in my memory—but she herself had not been recorded in this chain of mirages, and had she not told me her name herself, I would never in my life have remembered it. It was a name from the periphery of my circle of friends during the period just before I left Russia. I tried to remember all the occasions we might have met, but the faces blurred in my memory like a wine stain on a tablecloth sprinkled with salt. Maybe at Seva's. Or maybe at Senya's? Or even at Syoma's?

It could have been at any of a dozen of the places of those pre-departure, semi-dissident demi-brawls that began with furious ideological arguments after the first glass and ended with the hissing of a record forgotten on the gramophone, drowned by the roar of vomiting coming from the bathroom. A hot palm on the knee, confusion with coat sleeves, the rustling of a stocking under the skirt pulled up in a taxi, a deserted frost-covered street, and then the whirlwind of the bed and walls, the frenzied love battle, and finally the falling off, tuning out. More than once I would wake up in a strange apartment completely alone with a note on the kitchen table: "Gone to work. You'll call? The coffee's in the cupboard over the sink, eggs in the fridge." Where my brains were on mornings like that it was hard to say. I disappeared, I wouldn't call either the next day or the day after, and in a month I was no longer on the territory of the Soviet empire with its ideas about indissoluble love and eternal friendship.

The random geography of these farewell couplings had not imprinted itself on my memory; but I seemed to remember that upthrust chin and the bitten lip, and the windblown locks wet with melting snowflakes. Of course, there were rays of lines around the eyes focused by the magnifying glass of time on the bared temple; but she had practically not changed over all these years. Maybe the street lights which were now turning on in the dusk mummified her exterior with their waxy glow, but it seemed to me that, if she had not become younger, she had clearly grown prettier. I mentally undressed her right there on Gorky Street in the wet snow. She averted her gaze, and I blushed. "So when will we get together?" she asked, as if the fact of our meeting was not subject to debate and had been long since agreed upon. I, however, demurred: "I only have a week in Moscow. Relatives. And very close friends."

"And you mean we're not close friends anymore?"

I can't bear it when anyone doubts the greatness of my soul, the warmth of my heart, or my fidelity to my friends. A brave man is probably one who is prepared to look like a fool, a scoundrel, and a miser in public but at the same time not renege on either his attitudes or his itinerary. I want to be good, I want to be loved by everyone. And I followed her on that leash of guilt for not remembering my former lover. I even insisted on buying alcohol and cigarettes in the Intourist nearby, once again amazed that I was admitted to this forbidden zone, this temple of foreign currency, without being asked to show my British passport. She meanwhile went off to telephone, clearly to alert her friends.

In the taxi began that rhyming with the past: there was the rustling of the stocking and the drawn-up skirt, and the frozen

136

dark street rushed by as it had thirteen years ago. Embarrassed by pauses, I started talking about that displacement in time, how in Germany my trans-Europe train moved through the Eastern and Western sectors as if through different time zones, back and forth; you keep waking up from a dream and again falling into it, no longer understanding where the police and customs officers of the next passport control are coming from—from the delirium of half-sleep, or are they really checking your date of birth in the passport against the number of wrinkles on your face? When the train, that antediluvian time machine, finally crawled up to the Chop Station on the Soviet border, the station clock on the platform showed exactly zero zero hours zero zero minutes. The Soviet time system had taken over.

I entered the flat in the way a sick man comes to his senses and returns to the present after a sweaty delirium: slowly opening his bleary eyes and cautiously fumbling to touch forgotten objects with a weakened hand. This place was like a compartment in that long-distance railroad train—a train that had been shunted to a back track and left there for many years. Nothing had changed. The world around continued moving, this train continued standing, but inasmuch as the passengers never left the compartment, it seemed to them that their train was speeding, accelerating, departing the hateful world. I recognized separate items among its furnishings, and felt that sweet dizziness when the object that you touch with your hands coincides with the evasive image you had of it in memory. I remembered this night lamp with a stained-glass shade, and this knitted fringe of the tablecloth (as I had then, I threaded it through my fingers during embarrassing gaps in the conversation). And at the same time something irreparable took place that shifted and blurred the image of this room in my memory as on a broken television. I remembered the television set and the books on the wall to the right, but below the bookshelf something was clearly missing. Had there been an armchair there?

"I took away the fold-out bed after my mother died; as it is there's hardly room to move," she prompted, catching me blinking in doubt and confusion as I looked around the room. I naturally hadn't remembered (and probably didn't even know) that during all those years she lived with her mother. Judging by the way she twisted her lower lip and shrugged her shoulders (I remembered that grimace), she was clearly upset that I hadn't heard a thing about her mother's death. Only then did I notice a photograph in a frame with a mourning band: an enchanting face of a woman old beyond her years, deep-set eyes, thin lips, and a strong chin. I muttered some appropriately indistinct condolences, and, hiding my embarrassment, began with excessive vivacity to express surprise that we should have met after all these years at the cemetery, each of us by our mothers' graves. I stopped short. Thank God the doorbell rang, like break after a painful class.

The room quickly filled with semi-familiar faces. I thought that the blurriness of their features in my eyes was caused by years of exile numbing the memory of the past, although actually it was all the other way around: separation, like binoculars, sharpens the picture of memory. I'm sure that, had I stayed in Moscow, I would have recognized them with greater difficulty than I did now, so accidental were these people in my hectic life at the time. In order to hide my complete estrangement, I was exaggeratedly friendly, responded with a wink to every glance, answered every touch with a brotherly clap on the shoulder. Every new arrival looked me over as if I were a museum exhibit under glass. The glass was clearly there: it was as if they were afraid to touch me and were walking around me on tiptoe—the alarm might go off.

But there was also no end to the ecstatic sobs and shrieks,

accompanied by the refrain: "Look at him—he hasn't changed a bit!" While I could almost feel the brand of all the years of emigration on my skin, for them my experience didn't exist, and therefore for them there was no distance in time. I was totally theirs in that Moscow life, and all this was a continuation of my former relationships, telephone calls, correspondence; they didn't suspect the existence of another me they didn't know, a different one—from there. My London present, at that moment removed to some distant parallel that didn't intersect Moscow, was for them only a possible future, when all borders and dungeons would collapse. For them I remained the same as they remembered me: for me life here had stopped too when they remained behind the cordon. We all assigned each other a fictitious age.

We were still in the age group when, unless someone has gone bald or had a stroke, a person has not emigrated in appearance too far from his former thirty-year-old self. Our memory, our appearance, like our age, and like every feeling of faithfulness and devotion to some past, changes in bursts. After the first stiffness, the conversation with my old friends immediately took up again where it had left off thirteen years before. Time doesn't seem to exist in conversations—there is only place, the point of the dialogue where that conversation was interrupted. I benignly nodded my head to everyone around, vaguely realizing who I was talking to: "There is no time, there is only place." To which the hostess rejoined: "There's no place either, nowhere to sit down."

Scrutinizing the room filled to overflowing, I was again struck by the forgotten spirit of a Moscow gathering. Just an instant ago I had felt I was in an unfortunate country, aged beyond its years, doomed to stand with an outstretched hand at the crossroads of all civilizations. But that begging hand suddenly snapped its fingers and, as if produced from under a magician's coattails, the table shone with silver and dozens of dishes. Who cared that these were endless combinations of the same sour cabbage and potatoes with herring? The context, as always in Russia, was more important than the content. To prove the point, this content was disappearing with the same miraculous speed and inexplicability as it appeared on the table. The booze too disappeared with the same speed: the guests flocked into the apartment one after the other, each bottle they brought, and each hors d'oeuvre they would pick up, seemed to be the last and was therefore consumed instantly, in haste, at a single gulp. And in another instant there was no more dank and chilly darkness beyond the windowpane, but only the light and the human warmth emanating from the gathering around the table. However foreign these faces had seemed at first as they appeared in the doorway of this world, they were gradually becoming a part of the many-headed, many-armed being whose monstrous and dear features I knew well from former occasions. As if this apartment, like a religious sect, selected a particular physiological type of guest; the years passed, people changed, but not the set of their relationships, their breed, their clan. I no longer belonged to this clan. But I tried to hide this fact.

A foreigner in Russia is above the law, and a person with an exit visa in his pocket counted as a foreigner. At every drunken revel during my farewell days in Moscow, I would find gazes of adoration fixed on me. Repeating the predeparture rhythm, I was again undergoing this same cycle of delightfully senseless reveling, now, however, a certified foreigner with a passport. Someone put on an old record of Adamo Tombe la Neige, that same Adamo who was considered a symbol of everything French in the Moscow of the sixties, while in Paris, as it turned out, he was considered an Algerian. I caught that same adoring, ready-for-anything gaze from across the table, across the room. In part playing up to these eyes, in part as if justifying my presence among them like a child among adults, I began with vulgar haste (knowing the Moscow habit of interrupting) to entertain them with anecdotes and impressions of a foreign traveler in Russia. I had managed to describe the maniacal broadness of the streets—you can be born, marry, bring up your children, and die crossing Lenin Prospect or the Garden Ring; the lady who sells stinking sausage under the theater poster for Bulgakov's play, *Heart of a Dog*—what, you wonder, is the sausage made of? With particular gusto I told them about the Little Stage of the Children's Theater in my former house and about the warning to keep at least four meters away from the façade of my former dwelling, away from my past.

"Unlike you, we who stayed in Russia are deprived, to our great regret, of the possiblity of looking at our present as if from the outside," Eugenia pronounced, at a pause, from the other end of the table. I noticed that around the table they were exchanging glances. The bolder and wittier my tales were, the more malicious this exchange of glances would become. Apparently Eugenia's mournfully ironic response to my babble evoked in others the old refrain: emigration as betrayal. But I didn't realize that at the time, I only noted how Eugenia's face suddenly twisted—a wound of suffering, not a face; a wound not very carefully covered with Akhmatovian mournful aloofness and all-forgiving understanding. You over there, far from Moscow, from Russia, in the comfort of Western civilization, mired in materialism, have learned to look indifferently at the trials and tribulations that befall humanity; we, unfortunately, are deprived of that luxury; we, to our great regret, are obliged to devote ourselves entirely to spiritual resistance against the chaos and evil of this world.

"The past is a foreign country: they do things differently there," I quoted the English point of view, pretending that I hadn't noticed her poisonous irony. "It is essentially an émigré situation: you perceive the present life of your homeland nostalgically, as your own personal past." Again I rushed into an anecdote: about how a saleslady in the Intourist hotel, rejecting my credit card and demanding cash, pronounced in justification the macaronic phrase, mixing the two languages: "*Mashinka* broken." That's how the émigré Odessan Jews of New York's Brighton Beach talk. Now, it turns out, people talk like that in the most elegant hotels of Moscow where they take you for a well-to-do foreigner. The Soviet time *mashinka* was on the fritz. How terrifying the portals of these menacing buildings had once seemed—that zone forbidden to all ordinary Soviet mortals; it seemed as if the very fact of your Soviet origin, your citizenship had branded you as that ordinary mortal. And here I was walking past this ominous Cerberus the doorman, with his gold-trimmed cockade, without even showing my foreign passport, and he only bowed obsequiously with a vilely servile smile, not for a minute doubting my Intourist essence.

"Some of us would never think of going into these American Express hotel-motels whether they were allowed or not." They had bunched together in a sign of solidarity around Eugenia, so that in the course of the squabble it was sometimes hard for me to tell who of this great heap of young people (I suddenly found all of them particularly young and insolent) was talking to me. I had the feeling that whatever insults I received that evening were given at Eugenia's instigation: she reigned here not only as the hostess but as a revered supreme being whose least intentions were taken up by the crowd of sycophants and unquestioningly implemented. Whoever's lips moved, it was Eugenia's voice: "There are people who never even planned to leave the table, either to emigrate or to go into the underground. And who don't feel guilty of collaboration because they never participated in anything. There are people who don't think at all in terms of emigration, literature, and uncordonable freedom."

The word "uncordonable" sounded like "unpardonable": I was the embodiment of unpardonable freedom in their eyes. With all the greater unpardonableness they fixed their eyes on me, and gradually grew bolder: they emotionally stripped me on the spot. The central heating radiated a kind of bathhouse torpor, my tie choked me, and although sweat was pouring off my forehead, my throat was dry. I took off my jacket, threw it over the back of a chair, and out from it fell my British passport. Eugenia, sitting at the corner of the table, snatched it from the floor with unexpected agility, considering the drunken unintelligibility with which she had addressed me a moment earlier. Pulling her knees up under her, she settled herself in an armchair as if with a favorite book, leafing through my passport and inspecting its gilt insignia and the windows cut in the thick cover for name and number.

"Is it hard to get a thing like this?" she asked, as if it were some scarce object I'd bought by chance at a flea market. I began explaining about the four-year quarantine for residency and that finally you have to swear loyalty to the Queen. I knew that mentioning the oath to Her Majesty would get a rise out of the room: the idea of a knightly oath was as out of place in Moscow as strawberries in winter. Getting excited myself, I began recounting the well-rehearsed details of the procedure. How I entered the public notary's office of the City of London, and the Dickensian solicitor asked if I was prepared to swear on the Bible or would I simply pledge my allegiance to the Queen by juridical formula; how I said that I didn't want to take the defense of the Queen and her legal heirs upon myself personally, and therefore preferred to swear by God. He got out the Bible and read me the text of the oath which I was supposed to repeat, placing my hand on the Bible, thereby transferring the responsibility from my own shoulders to God's, I thought. But I said that although I wanted to dispense with my personal responsibility, that I couldn't place it on the shoulders of a foreign God.

"What do you mean, a foreign God? In what sense foreign?" Eugenia interrupted me, not immediately understanding. The lawyer had also not understood immediately. Then he understood and ran around his office looking for an Old Testament, the Jewish one, of the Bible. Got it? He found only one of the books and said, "I can't find the whole thing—will a part do?" I said that even a line of the Holy Writ would do. He said that Exodus and Prophets were in this volume. Would that do? Of course it would do! What else could I swear on in my émigré situation if not on the book of Prophets and the story of the flight out of Egypt?

"So it's not enough for you that you're a Jew—you want to join the Queen's musketeers besides?" came the voice from the other end of the table. I lowered my head and, not knowing what to answer, fingered the fringe of the tablecloth. Before my eyes arose, unchanged all these years, the greasy wallpaper with the torn border, the plates of mushroom ends and sardine tails, the rough calico of the split oilcloth apron on the doorknob in the kitchen, and in the bathroom—hairs stuck in the soap bar by the sink next to the rusty squeezed-out toothpaste tube. All this merged into one squalor along with the bags under the eyes and the extended wrinkled necks of my former countrymen. The more vividly I spoke about the exoticism there, about my oath, the barristers, the Bible, and the Queen's power in general, the more clearly the moral of my English fairy tales could be read in their eyes: "So you're special, and we here are the same old Soviet dumb pricks?"

"So what do you all come here for? To have a look at how we're screwing up?" She twisted her lower lip and pulled up her shoulders. Obscenities in her mouth sounded affected and artificial, but not like an insult directed at me, but rather like demonstrative scorn for herself: I've been around, I'm no simpleton, I won't beat around the bush, I've got nothing to be ashamed of.

"Maybe there's no point in playing the Bacchante?" her neighbor at the table warned her cautiously, watching her throw back another shot of vodka. She was half lying, with her chest on the table as if it were the counter of a bar, propping up her head on her arm bent at the elbow: from the chin thrust upward, the expression of her eyes seemed haughty, especially when she lazily clicked her fingernails against her teeth. In the theatrical lighting of the night light with its shade of colored glass in one corner and the dim lamp in the other, her face became younger and more insolent, a vague smile curved her lips with increasing insistence. She, like the rest of the guests, sat in the tropical climate of this overheated Moscow apartment in almost summery clothing, and I saw up inside her wide, folded-back sleeve her strong white shoulder and unshaved armpit.

"You came here to see what a monster you used to be in your Soviet life? To look at us through the bars of our cage in the zoo: we're still apes, and you're already *homo sapiens*? But the metamorphoses and cataclysms we go through, I assure you, are no less earthshaking, though they're not as visible to outsiders. I work in an institute of gerontology. We do experiments. I know. The heart of a mouse beats as many times in a lifetime as an elephant's. Of course the elephant lives much longer. But the mouse's heart beats faster."

"Russia for some reason has always, like Chekhov's widow, made herself out to be a poor, helpless creature," I finally decided to answer. Her morally instructive tone began to get on my nerves. "This elephant keeps on pretending to be a mouse."

"It doesn't matter who's the mouse and who's the elephant. It's just that what looks like the fuss of a mouse was for us the terrifying tread of rhinoceroses."

145

It was no accident that the word "mouse" had come up: the conversation was, of course, unconsciously not about mice but about rats. About rats abandoning a sinking ship. Because the conversation was a repetition of the kitchen arguments of thirteen years ago when I, about to go into emigration, sat just like this before the prosecuting faces of my countrymen. Then Russia had been compared not with an elephant and not with a mountain bringing forth a mouse, but with a sinking ship. But no decent person then dared to compare the emigrants with rats. Because everyone suspected that besides the rats running from a sinking ship there were also underground rats, sitting it out in the corners.

"We're not talking about Russia in general," she rejected any attempt at compromise as if she were sweeping crumbs from the table. "We're talking about us, sitting at the table, about my circle of friends, about the ones who stayed here. Who went through all the hell of the last decade. You represent yourself as a new man. But look at us carefully: have we really not changed? Look at what we've turned into. This terror that turns you inside out transforms a person. You can't imagine what's been going on here." She turned to the curtained window—hiding tears?

"Have you read about the Vietnamese refugees who were fed to the sharks? About the Khmer Rouge? Mountains of rotting corpses!" There was nothing left for me to do but to defend myself with the same weapon: who had suffered more. "Listening to you, you'd think Russia had a monopoly on suffering."

"It's quite possible that the Khmer Rouge are worse than the Bolsheviks. I'm not talking about that. I'm talking about the uniqueness of our suffering. I simply mean that the last decade of Russian terror could not have been deduced from previous experience. A person outside Russia is therefore unable to understand what we have had to understand."

146

"I have always felt that the idolization of suffering was a cynical and hypocritical tendency. At best it is a pretext to avoid any decisive steps to rid oneself of suffering," I paused, and finally decided to cut myself off entirely from the idea that we shared a common lot: "In short, I'm not a Christian and I don't think that the path to truth is through suffering." That's why I left Russia and you stayed, I was about to say, but restrained myself in time.

"You're very naive, Zinovy," she smiled condescendingly. "You think that we chose whether or not to suffer. You think we have a choice at all. I'll tell you something," and for the first time in the whole conversation she looked me in the eye. "Every person has to die. But besides that natural end, each of us sooner or later dies another death, a kind of metamorphosis, like Saul's into Paul. This can be by conversion to another religion or, the reverse, by prison and exile, or perhaps by emigration. It can be a completely ordinary act, but one that changes the whole course of your life. And after this death, you understand that it is impossible to change anything. And there's no choice. And you are alone." And she looked away again.

"You wanted to say something to me," I murmured.

"I wanted to say that despite all your fateful peregrinations and perturbations, you have not experienced this second, or rather, this first and most important death. What's more, I have the impression that you don't even suspect its existence."

"You mean that all of you here are already dead and only I am alive?" I got up, knocking over my glass. "Well then, lie here, little corpses. But I'm going."

I got up. I saw how Eugenia's eyes in hypocritical embarrassment at my outburst began wandering guiltily around the room. I was here because of her and for her; I paused, giving her a last chance to divert this verbal assault from the well-trodden path of the Russian sense of guilt and complicity. I expected she would make some small gesture or say a word that would return the conversation to everyday pleasant and humorous small talk. I looked around from one of them to the next, reading in their faces only one simple thought: everything in the world was so dreadful that nothing good could exist. I existed. That meant there was nothing good in me. Getting caught in the sleeves of my coat, I quietly closed the door behind me. ("I'm running away again, I'm avoiding responsibility again, I should have stayed, should have proved to them, proved to myself . . ." I muttered, taking three steps at a time down the dark stairway towards the exit.)

She caught up with me on the last landing. She flew down the stairs like a boisterous schoolgirl skidding on the slippery tiles and stopped stone still. She was out of breath. A dim smeared bulb over the elevator door was the only source of light; the grilled gate of the lift, reflected in the dark spattered window, gave the geography of this stairway cage a literal cage-like feeling, like that of a prison or a zoo. There was no exit. And because the external walls were indestructible and there was no possibility of breaking out, one wanted to break down the emotional fence between us, to break the machine, the mechanism of pretense and pose, and look at what was inside. In the waxy yellow light her face lost any signs of age, like an Egyptian mask. In the heat of love the years merge and the difference in ages disappears, as at conception the ages of the parents are merged. Time stops for a moment and therefore stops existing at all. With every second I was falling out of time and geography. Like a blind man knowing by heart the way from the bus stop to the entry of his home, my hand recognized her body even in the roughness of her rustling stocking, while my tongue overcame the temporal distance of separation, imitating the movement of her tongue, as in a half-forgotten and complicated ballroom dance known by the partner. She climbed onto the window sill in an absurd ballet arabesque, with her arms around my neck, and whispered in my ear about how she had waited for me and knew that I would certainly come one day "to have a look at me and see how I have changed."

At that moment a door burst open above and the noise from the apartment rolled down along the stairway. She huddled up to me like a girl on the platform when a freight train passes. "What about your friends upstairs?" I asked mechanically, filling the pause, while my hand circled her body like a blind beggar circling familiar streets, bumping into obstacles known in advance. "I'm sick of all of them," she murmured in answer, helping my hand to escape from deceptive blind alleys. "I know that we are right and you are wrong, I'm ready to sign every word, but I don't need to be right, I want to be with you here, there, wherever. I wasn't arguing with you. It was a declaration of love, didn't you understand?" During this whispering she had thrown herself back on the window sill, encircled me, standing, as if growing into me with her hips, while my hands got lost in her pulled-up dress and my lips moved downwards, pushing along her lips, neck, breasts. I seemed to recognize the taste of her lips, and the uneven pellet of her nipple. With a kind of adolescent frenzy I tried to penetrate through her to my former years of debaucheries and hopes, when a debauchery was a test of the hope of endurance, faithfulness, and patience, and therefore, a pledge of optimism. I tried to prove to her by my impetuosity that I hadn't changed at all, that I was the same as I was then, in those nights of pre-departure revelry. Her bra snapped, her stocking tore, she cried out when I crossed the boundaries of her body.

She threw herself back and stopped resisting. Her hand, tightened in a fist on the window sill, began to unclench and opened like a flower. Between her fingers a key slipped from her open palm. My tongue continued its unintelligible dialogue with the tongue I encountered, but I couldn't take my eyes off the key with its pendant. The pendant was foreign, a souvenir brought to Moscow from a trip abroad or a present from a tourist, a cheap thing like glass beads for the natives. But that coarse amulet on the chipped window sill of a Moscow entryway for a moment distorted the sense of geography in my mind, reminding me of London. Knickknacks like that sell from the souvenir stalls on Trafalgar Square, where police helmets of black plastic lie next to mugs painted like the British flag, as well as these same pendants in the shape of a guardsman with a cocked hat, cockade and shakos, capes and shoulder-knots, and all made of colored lead, like a pewter toy soldier from childhood, a portion of British patriotism weighed out on a scale accessible to tourists. Back in the mid-1970s, just before I left Moscow, a foreign correspondent there had given me a little soldier just like this one. As if it had been abandoned here by me to the enemy's mercy, the guardsman on the key ring dangled now from its chain, swaying like a hanged man from the window sill.

I recalled the real Queen's beefeater on duty by the gates of the Horse Guard on a bright golden October day when the falling ripe chestnuts would bounce like children's balls off the asphalt, and the pigeons on Trafalgar Square would fly off with every strike of Big Ben. The guardsman was always imperturbable: he wouldn't twitch a whisker, even when a child from the provinces would pull on his musket, or a wheat-colored Swedish girl would kiss him on the cheek while a Japanese tourist photographed her. But I'm not a tourist in London; I walk along with the same boring imperturbability with which the Queen's guardsman scrutinizes the tourist hubbub around him. How wonderful after the hell of the editorial hustle to find oneself at sunset in a quiet pub with oak panelling where anonymous cigar smoke creeps furtively from behind the bar, and through the ripples of a blown-glass screen you can see a female face singing in a slightly hoarse voice two or three indistinguishable blues phrases about the sadness of life and separation.

What am I doing here on this spittle-covered landing in a city I once left, never to return to? There is no return to a lover once abandoned: love for a woman is as unique as life itself, which is given but once. A relapse of love from the same person is a fatal illness. In some fraction of a second I felt I would never get out of here again, that I could never prove that I belonged to the British crown. The cashmere overcoat would wear out quickly, the elbows of the Scottish tweed jacket wear through, the soles of the English leather shoes tear, and I would once again become indistinguishable from the rest of the Soviet crowd.

I finally remembered that drunken night thirteen years ago: it matured in my memory like French brandy. We drank everything, matured or not, but with a high alcohol content. Those dashes in taxis from one flat to the next, the metro tunnel, again bright light, a table with canned goods and vodka, and a furious argument with her friends about guilt and complicity inside and out of prison walls (or the Soviet borders?); I get up, swaying and bumping against the walls, run down the stairs, she after me, dragging me back to the apartment, and crashing down in the semi-darkness onto the bed we battle like two angels, as if again trying to force each other to think differently. I remembered how I awakened in the middle of that night not knowing where I was.

"Zhenka, where are you?" The voices of the crowd of merrymaking guests we'd abandoned resounded inside the stairway cage. I saw my own face reflected in the window together with the prison bars of the lift doors behind me. "Zhenka? Do you hear? We're sick of waiting. We're leaving."

She started, pushed away from me, and the pewter soldier of the Queen's guard slipped off the window sill. He fell, hitting the tiles with a dull clank. She raised herself from the window sill leaning on an elbow, her dress unbuttoned, a lock of hair fallen to her shoulder together with the undone clip. Embarrassed, I pulled away from her and, bending down quickly, picked up the guardsman from the slimy tiles. I stood before her, holding the little soldier in my fist, and gazed at her, straining my sight in the dim waxy light, not certain that her face was identical to the familiar image that suddenly flashed through my mind.

"Zhenka, where are you? We're going," voices again resounded from the top of the stairs accompanied by the slamming of doors and the thudding of feet. I remembered how I had awakened on that unfortunate night not knowing where I was and, crawling out of bed, hit my head painfully on the bookshelf. I remembered how, half-naked in my shirt, I made my way to the toilet, blindly groping for direction in the pitch darkness. How, clearly having mixed up the doors, I found myself in a room I hadn't known existed. The street lamp illuminated the window sill powdered on the outside with snow. On a bed by the window sat a young girl, with a thrust-out chin and sullen look. She looked as if she'd been sitting in that position all night. I had clearly confused the room, if not the city and the century. In confusion I fumbled at the buttons of my shirt, trying to cover my naked chest; my hand struck something hard in my breast pocket, and I pulled out the pewter soldier—the Queen's guardsman, the London souvenir, the present given to me by a Moscow correspondent of the *Times*. I stood there, twisting him aimlessly in my hands, and then I held him out to the girl on the bed, as a kind of foolish peace-token, *bakshish* for the involuntary intrusion. The pewter soldier fell on the sheet as if struck by an invisible bullet;

she reached out to him and laid him on her open palm like a dead baby bird.

The illuminated glass box of the lift floated downwards filled with Eugenia's guests who had given up waiting for their hostess. The checkered light of the elevator cage, like a net, fell on the pewter soldier; she again squeezed him in her fist as if realizing that she had revealed too much to an outside eye. The faces of my recent opponents descended smoothly in the lift, appraising us through the barred glass with a squeamish glance as if we were unpleasant representatives of exotic fauna in a zoo. In a minute the door of the lift crashed below and a voice rung out: "It's a crisis of desire. Have you noticed our young girls have stopped being friends with their contemporaries? They go after their elders, scorn their own generation. They want something ready-made, middle-aged, tried and tested. They don't wish to dare. A crisis of desire. Disgusting!" And the outside door slammed, screeching on its heavy springs.

"You had a daughter," I finally made up my mind and voiced my suspicions aloud. "On that last night I saw your daughter in the next room. Where is she, what it she doing?"

I looked at her lips, ravaged by my attempts to destroy the distance in time between our two meetings, gazed into her eyes that were trying to avoid mine. In her features I now recognized the face of her daughter that I had seen many years ago. Like the future in the past: the daughter recognized in the mother. And the features of the mother looking out of the face of the daughter are the past in the future. I had forgotten not only that she had a mother, but that she had a daughter. Returning to your native city is a summons to the draft board of history: you seemed to have left the ranks, to be on eternal leave, outside time, without the problem of fathers and children, ancestors and progeny. But one step across the border and they start taking down your passport particulars: height, eye color, and your age, your age, your age. Your watch is fast. And yours is slow. But mine has stopped.

I recalled the photograph of her mother in the apartment: the gaunt and exhausted, but charming face of a woman a little over forty years old. How old had her mother been then? Eugenia was my age, about thirty, when our paths crossed; that means that now, thirteen years later, she had caught up to her mother in the photograph.

But Eugenia didn't look over forty, even in the deadening waxy light of the stairwell. She looked the way she had frozen in my memory for thirteen years: thirty years old. It was her daughter who should be about thirty, whose room I had wandered into thirteen years ago in a drunken state without pants and with a pewter Queen's guardsman in my fist.

"What daughter?" She raised her eyebrows. "I am the daughter. You even gave me this pendant, don't you remember? But Mama died. Cancer. Gave up waiting for a letter from you. You promised to send us an invitation so that we could apply for an exit visa. Don't you remember? Forget it. We decided later not to emigrate anyway. Shall we go upstairs?"

1990

Translated by Priscilla Meyer

THE FACE OF THE AGE

IN MY MIND'S EYE, I ALWAYS PICTURE MY CHILDHOOD bathed in a twofold light. On the one hand, there is the light of communism, words of optimism from a radio permanently switched on, informing me that there was no other land where a man could breathe so freely. The rhythmic swish of bouncy bicycle tires on asphalt roads, scorching hot in the summer noonday; the blissful smell of hot bread rolls and boiled potatoes, with a herring on Sundays. The whiff of a newly-ironed pioneer scarf in my nostrils; the tickling of a starched white shirt, pressed by my mother, as school began again after summer camp. My heart thumps as I look forward to meeting my schoolfriends: has anybody grown an inch taller? The chiming of the tramcar bell has all the piercing thrill of a glass of champagne, or the scent of orange peel at New Year. The crunch of poplar-catkins beneath the soles of polished shoes, the roll call of our voices in the back yard, as we chase after a stray cat by the dustbin shed. The way it would hiss and snarl, tail erect, when we closed round it in a tight circle: everyone with a stone in his fist and a sweet lump in his throat from the May air gulped in as he ran. Then the soundless twitching of a creature battered to death by the hail of stones. A rivulet of perspiration runs down my spine between the shoulder blades. Like the merited relaxation of an old Bolshevik, a drowsy noonday at my school desk, as the textbooks slip from my fingers to the monotonous repetition of clopping hooves, the admonitions of teachers, and the cry of the junk man outside the window. All this I carry with me into the bright future.

But parallel with that cloudless Soviet paradise, there existed a quite other world in my childhood—a world of shadows, secret, magical. This world would appear in our doorway crowned by the tiara of Aunt Irena's auburn curls. They cascaded endlessly onto her bare shoulders, as if hastening in embarrassment to cover up the décolletage of her black watered-silk dress, as black as the lustrous starry night on the record sleeve she held in her hand. From the cellophane sheen of this foreign-manufactured black square, the mirror image of Aunt Irena gazed at us. With a long *papirosa* between her scarlet lips, she seemed to float on the golden fleece of her hair above cosmic deeps, where the smoke dissolved into stardust. My father took this gramophonic marvel from Aunt Irena the way the first Soviet emigrants took their exit visas: it was material evidence of the other world. While he was winding up the record player, the whole family seated themselves round the table beneath the green lampshade. The Crimean port in the crystal decanter sprayed crimson reflections onto the fringed brocade tablecloth, and the green rings from the shade, framing every glass, were no more than theatrical properties and footlights for the golden fleece of Aunt Irena's hair. I can see her, propping her chin, with a "Flowers of Herzegovina" *papirosa* in her scarlet lips: her eyes are slightly narrowed, perhaps from the cigarette smoke, or perhaps also because she was gazing too intently into the abyss of the black hole in the record, trying to make out unearthly images, not accessible to us mere mortals. She is smiling mysteriously to herself, like the lady on the record. But when the needle began to hiss, the blissful sounds of mysterious words came pouring out from under the green abyss of the lampshade. What language it was, I had no idea. My childish knowledge of geography boiled down to the fact that Red Square was the center of the earth. I do believe I had never in my life heard this bewitching combination of guttural twittering and melodious squealing. Was it Croat or Maltese? Tibetan or Catalan? What mattered was that this tongue had no connection whatever with our ordinary Soviet means of communication.

"Irenka, darling, we're waiting," Mama reminded her in a whisper, as she emerged from her dream of ecstasy. Aunt Irena, like her double on the glossy record sleeve, was a creature not of this earth: she knew a foreign language—that meant she had access to other worlds. She swept a slow glance of surprise round the table, as if she were seeing us all for the first time. With a shake of her golden fleece of hair, she spoke, as though returning to the sublunary world and its denizens.

"Can one imagine translating that divine simplicity into Russia? Poetry, after all, is what gets lost in translation," she said, shaking her head as she answered her own question. "There is nothing in this song reminiscent of our depressing way of life. A different vocabulary. Beauty. Love. Freedom. Words alien to our poverty-stricken, false existence!" She extinguished her *papirosa,* savagely crumbling the unsmoked tobacco into the ashtray.

"Why false? Why poverty-stricken?" said her husband, Uncle Arkady, wringing his hands and fidgeting on his chair. "We spent quite a nice August on the Black Sea. Chicken Kiev. See the Crimean port there. Then there's the gramophone. Caviar, thank the Lord. We don't stint ourselves, I'll have you know." In response, Aunt Irena merely fluttered her eyelashes, as a society lady might twirl her fan.

"Don't rock your chair, Arkady," said Mama, seizing the chance to catch her brother-in-law out.

"A false and poverty-stricken existence," repeated Aunt Irena, like a refrain, echoing the voice on the record. This time she shook her mop of curls mutinously, like a horse's mane, and crossed her legs in their patterned stockings, one knee over the other. Father averted his eyes, sighing heavily as he

157

jumped up from the table and began furiously to turn the handle of the gramophone.

"It's your stomach, Irena," pronounced Granddad categorically. He was profoundly convinced that all mankind's ills, from the Pharaohs to the Führer, had their seat in poor digestion. He understood a bilious nature to mean literally an excess of bile. An ordinary doctor by profession, he had stood all his life behind his chemist's counter; nevertheless in his heart, he reckoned himself a pharmaceutical genius, something in the nature of a medieval alchemist. He spent all his spare time inventing a panacea for every stomach ailment. Each newly invented recipe (known in our domestic circle as mixum-pixum-compositum) was tried out in the first instance on Grandma or the dachsund. Presently the dachsund died— this tragic event coincided, I now understand, with Stalin's doctors plot—and the neighbors whispered that Grandfather had done the dog to death with his chemical experiments. Grandma furiously rebutted these rumors, pointing out that she, as they could see, was as large as life; she ate her stewed fruit with the best, despite having swallowed a lifetime's worth of Grandfather's potions, certainly no less than the dachsund had. The animal had simply succumbed to the epidemic of rabies which was raging in Moscow that year.

"Poison or rabies, what difference does it make? One thing's plain: even the dog couldn't resign itself to the falsity and poverty of our existence."

"As to that, we could buy a new poodle, if need be. Or a lap dog. We don't stint ourselves," Uncle Arkady shrugged irritably.

"You shouldn't teach the boy to look on the dark side of things," Mama said in support of Uncle Arkady, while Grandma took the opportunity to slip me another portion of curd fritters and sour cream: she regarded misfortune (and any falling-out came under that heading) as something to be warded off with filling foodstuffs. I detested curd fritters with sour cream and adored Aunt Irena's golden fleece; looking on the dark side of things in general, and the death of our dachsund in particular, excused an absence of appetite and served as a pretext for refusing the fritters. I therefore demonstratively shared Aunt Irena's gloom, although I was really an incorrigible optimist. Deep down, I considered that I was living in the happiest country on earth, and was shocked every time my father sat himself next to Aunt Irena with the same perpetual questioning. "Tell me, Irenochka, what is this abroad of yours? What does it look like? The streets? The people? The houses?" He would put this question an untold number of times, with the fervor of a child imploring its parents to tell a familiar fairy story before bed. And Aunt Irena, in a slowed-down, almost dreamlike fashion, would emphatically light up yet another *papirosa*. Then, narrowing her eyes, partly from the smoke and partly from the instantaneous clarity of her recollection of a lost paradise, she would repeat, like a poem, one and the same thing every time.

"Well now, how can I put it? The exact words, I mean. If one could experience freedom and happiness, beauty and love just by describing them in words, we wouldn't need freedom, happiness, beauty, or love, would we?" And she would fix her veiled gaze on the window, weeping in the February thaw. "How to stand back from a moveable feast and describe it in mere words? An endless variety of manners, dress, and faces. The profusion of consumer goods. You sit at your pavement café table and that whole joyous, motley, diverse world swirls around you. And you begin to swirl with it." She would get up from the table: high heels, patterned stockings, close-fitting watered silk with a plunging neckline. The gold of her curls, spilling over her bare shoulders, looked to me from below, with the height of a little boy, like a rising sun as she bent down and took me in her arms and began waltzing me round the room. And Papa would invite Mama, and Granddad Grandma, to join the dance.

Only Uncle Arkady would shake his head forlornly, and grumble: "Well, what of it? We've got places of public entertainment too. What about our Gorky Park?"

This idyll, of course, could not last for ever. One fine day, Aunt Irena was whisked away in an automobile to an unknown destination. "Where have they taken Aunt Irena?" I asked. "It's her stomach," explained Grandfather. What had happened to her was something the grown-ups whispered about in corners; as soon as I appeared they would shut up, or start communicating by way of cryptic hints. Still, at times things did go further than mere hints. Uncle Arkady would clutch his head. "She has compromised the reputation of our whole family in the eyes of Soviet public opinion." Crushed, Papa would mumble: "That's something that could happen to anyone these days." "Go on, say it: the falsity and poverty of our existence was to blame for her moral failings," Mama would retort acidly. "A person who respected family ties wouldn't have entered into a criminal liaison like that," Uncle Arkady agreed. "You don't believe in stinting yourself either, do you?" said my father, stabbing an irate glance at him. Aunt Irena's name was evidently taboo for several months, until it transpired that far from the bustle of the world—in the mysterious land of stellar deeps of the gramophone records, as I supposed—she had taken some fateful decision without consulting her relations.

"We don't stint ourselves, but there is such a thing as conscience," Uncle Arkady gritted.

"Conscience, Arkady, is something your spouse lost during her trips abroad," confirmed Mama. "She did pick up something else, though."

"You might have some sympathy: she came within a hairsbreadth of dying of it," said Father, indignant.

These ominous allusions on the part of the grown-ups concerning Aunt Irena's unseemly conduct did not alter my attitude towards her, because for me she was poetry itself, and just as in poetry content is identical with form, so her moral outlook was, for me, identical with her outward appearance. At night in my dreams I would swim after that golden fleece, the waves alternately lifting me to the heights and drawing me down into the depths, until I realized that these waves were actually Aunt Irena's curls. The golden fleece of my dream pilgrimage to fairyland was within my grasp: taut, yet buoyant, it bore me onward to the promised shore.

But when Aunt Irena returned, at length, to hearth and home, and I saw those curls once again with my own eyes, they seemed to have lost their former foxy sleekness, the hypnotic luster of my dreams. On the other hand, they had become more abundant, thicker and wheaten, like the grain harvest on Soviet posters. From force of habit, she would still wearily draw back a stray tress from her forehead, but now her fingers picked anxiously at her hair as if checking to see that everything was as it should be, that the grain-bins had not been robbed of a single ear of corn.

Aunt Irena's return from her "trip abroad" had been like an awakening, just as unexpected for me as her disappearance had been. She, like her hair, remained as before, but at the same time, somehow different. Or had I perhaps, over those few months, changed from boy to adolescent, and begun to look at her with different eyes? She still wore her watered-silk dress with the low neckline in the evenings, but its dark colors had begun to look like mourning—for whom, it was unclear.

"All that money tossed away for nothing. Sheer waste," Uncle Arkady wrung his hands, as he sipped at Mama's borsch. He was taking his meals with us more and more often, as Aunt Irena had ceased to bother with such vulgar and worldly matters as housekeeping. "It's her stomach," Granddad reassured us. On solemn family occasions, she seemed drowsy and abstracted. She would sit mutely in front of her untouched glass of port and no longer sought to find words to describe the endless variety of manners, faces, and consumer goods to be found abroad. She no longer brought us the record with the glossy beauty, and Father no longer wound up the gramophone. He just kept on impressing something on her in a severe voice. No longer did the whole family twirl together in the dance. The only foreign twitterings we sometimes heard came from her room, where she had hauled our gramophone and would sit half-dressed in front of the mirror, combing her hair with a frenzy that bid fair to straighten out her curls for good. Sometimes I got the impression she was overdoing the luxurious procedure purely for my benefit.

On one occasion, however, I caught a glimpse through the half-open door of my father, running his hands through her hair. I heard his deep voice but was unable to decipher the words. Noticing me in the doorway, she beckoned me to her and lowered her head to let me reach the silken waves where I had so often drowned in dreams. "Have a feel," she said and let my fingers probe still deeper into her golden mane of hair. "You like that? And you're not frightened? You're not afraid of the truth?" I didn't understand what she wanted of me, and I trembled unaccountably. Papa, with a forlorn gesture, left the room and slammed the door. Aunt Irena pressed me still closer to her hair: it didn't smell of wheat, rather of daisies or stardust. "The truth, my boy, can be ugly and dreadful, can't it? You're really not afraid?" If I had been afraid of the truth, I still wouldn't have been able to put my fear into words: my lips were already out of my depth in that paradise of curls. I was merely shaking, but by no means out of fear. At that moment, my mother burst in and hauled me out of the room, yelling either to my father or Aunt Irena: "What are you trying to do—scar the boy for life?"

This mysterious threat of psychological trauma began to be repeated at every important date in my country's history. At such times I became a nervous and suspicious child, because whispering in corners, obscure hints, and equivocal behavior on the part of the grown-ups compelled me to be perpetually on the alert: I learned to guess at secret meanings where they might not have existed. In this context, it was only natural that the day of Stalin's funeral should intrigue me, because on that somber occasion a minute's silence was announced across the whole country: by now I knew from experience how significant a role conversational pauses played in my family. I had been promised that, for a whole minute, the country would fall silent, freeze, subside into immobility. The factories would fall silent, the trams come to a halt, pedestrians become rooted to the spot. I went outside in good time, so as not to miss the magical moment when, before my very eyes, everything living on the earth would become dead, only to revive an instant later. However, I was not to see it.

I distinctly remember that the minute's silence found me on the corner of October Street. I was most certainly there when the factories fell silent, the trams came to a halt, and the pedestrians froze by the traffic lights. But I didn't perceive all this as a minute of silence—I failed to enter some other world at that moment. At that instant, I was engaged in an argument with a soda-water seller on the corner. She just went on squirting the stuff as if nothing else was happening, obviously ignoring the inevitable approach of the fateful minute. "You could endanger the minute's silence," I told her in a menacing tone. I could tell she was going to carry on pouring the soda water into the glass (so that all the effervescence wouldn't disappear in the course of the minute). The liquid would hiss and bubble, thus breaking into the silence. In fact, it was drowned out not by the hissing but by the foul language of the seller, when she started telling me where to go with my minute's silence. Or perhaps I took the mournful factory sirens for car hooters, and the general traffic halt coincided with a red light? However it actually was, I missed the minute of silence, let it slip by, bungled the whole thing.

I went back home in floods of tears. I immediately realized that, in our house, the silence had been ignored on principle. The place was full of noise and the clinking of glasses: the blasphemous atmosphere of a family party held sway. A whole banquet, improvised by Grandma, was on the table. Boiled potatoes steamed away with public-spirited zeal, herring peered in astonishment through onion-ring spectacles, red caviar blushed in an ecstasy of embarrassment, a chilled bottle of vodka lay soaking the napkin. Then the champagne cork went flying up to the ceiling, and the grown-ups clinked their glasses together, congratulating one another on the death of "that mustachioed cockroach". True, Uncle Arkady attempted to make a speech about fidelity to the communist ideals and Leninist standards of Party life, distorted by Stalinism. Father, however, would not let him finish and struck up at full blast with "O tyrants, progeny of vice", from *Rigoletto*.

I was so alarmed by this inappropriate rejoicing that I clung to Aunt Irena's knees: she was the only one of the family not to share in this impious exultation over the death of the Leader and Teacher of all times and peoples. Surely this was the reason she was wearing neither the low-cut watered-silk dress, nor the patterned stockings and high-heeled shoes. Her neck, elongated now with the years, was enclosed in a high-buttoned collar. Dressed like that, she looked like a eyeglass-case. I fancied that she had observed her one minute's silence, contemplating, with sorrowful indifference, the other members of the family peppering the ceiling with champagne corks in their infantile irresponsibility. When everybody had calmed down a little, Father sat down beside Aunt Irena and tried to make her see things in a more optimistic light, to stir her interest in public life in the context of crumbling prisons and monuments of Stalinism.

"And on the shards of Tsardom's grandeur, Our names will shine out side by side," declaimed Uncle Arkady by way of explanation, washing a sprat sandwich down with champagne. "By hell, the poet was right! We needn't stint ourselves when it comes to celebration."

"Does the death of one person release the whole country from its inner falsity? How about the dungeons of the heart? The deep cellars of our conscience?" enquired Aunt Irena rhetorically, with the pessimism and aloofness of a rejected oracle, refusing to succumb to the hypnosis of universal optimism.

"You want the whole Politburo to bite the dust, do you? Ha!" Uncle Arkady clutched his head. But Aunt Irena ignored these provocative demands. Similar scenes continued to be repeated at every stage of the subsequent thaw. Even the Twentieth Party Congress, unmasking the cult of personality, left her cold.

"Surely you can see the face of our homeland changing before your very eyes," a perplexed Uncle Arkady would say. "You must acknowledge, Irenchik, that we have at last got rid of the cult in us, which has darkened the minds of millions."

Aunt Irena, twirling a tress of her lackluster golden fleece with an exhausted gesture, would reply: "What have the minds of millions to do with me? What about the private secrets in the gloomy cellars of the memory?"

"As for opinions, we don't stint ourselves in any way," persisted Uncle Arkady. "You won't deny that our family has finally rid itself of fear."

"Family? Rid itself? From fear?" Aunt Irena repeated acidly, and directed her narrowed gaze at Father. Mother also tried to catch Father's eye, finger pointing to temple, glancing sideways at Aunt Irena. For some reason, Father usually kept quiet during arguments of this sort, but at this he burst out:

"What is it you're after, Irena? What do you want all of us to do? Do you want to destroy the family?" Aunt Irena rose from her armchair, but Mama rushed to intercept her.

"You don't understand, Mishenka," she said to Father in a tearful little-girl voice. With an ingratiating smile, she took Aunt Irena's arm, and tried to pilot her out of the room. "And you, Irishkin, why be like this? Really now. Don't go on behaving this way, I implore you. For the child's sake. Surely you don't want him scarred for life?"

"Quite the contrary," replied Aunt Irena, deftly freeing herself from Mama's embrace. "It's for our children's sake that we must have done with this hypocrisy, this inner falsehood, these ignoble charades of conscience." She bent down to me and cupped my face in her palms. Gazing into my eyes, she asked: "Do you love me? As I am? And do you want to know the truth?" I shook my head, remembering Mama's shrieks about scarring children. "If you find out the truth, you won't stop loving me?" she asked, as the family wrangle reached an ominous pause. My parents, tense and motionless, were divided from us by the green light of the lampshade, now more unearthly than cozy.

I was too afraid to budge. I didn't want to know her secret. I reckoned secrets ought to be kept to oneself. It was more interesting that way. What the secret was didn't matter in the least. As children, we used to bury all kinds of strange things in the back yard and cover the hole up with a piece of glass:

under that glass pane any sort of rubbish, like colored candy wrappers or pebbles, looked like a real treasure trove. Of course I felt rather fearful about being present at family cross-examinations, with all the pauses and innuendoes, winkings and whisperings in corners, but on the other hand I had seen how "ignoble charades of conscience" were transforming Aunt Irena into an all-powerful creature: everybody deferred to her, trying to discover what was in her mind. No wonder they kept trying to find out what it was she wanted. She was the possessor of a solemn mystery, a family secret. The longer they tried to conceal this secret from me, the more convoluted their conversations became—and, as I guessed, their attitudes to one another as well. The more absurd and puzzling the secret, the more absorbing and difficult it becomes to keep the thing quiet, the more stories are needed to deflect the interest of the inquirer.

Possibly this domestic atmosphere made me all the more prone to create secrets for myself, things which needed safe-guarding. Thus, I had occasion to lie resourcefully to my parents. Not always very resourcefully, however, and not always to conceal a secret. Not to put too fine a point on it, I started lying without any pretext, and without any particular logical end in view. I became a pathological fibber. I remember sitting in front of the television chewing on an orange. "What's that you're chewing?" my father asked, as he walked in. "An apple," I said without blinking. "Why tell lies?" my father enquired. I didn't know: so as not to tell the truth, evidently. "I'm not," I replied. "Why tell lies that you're not telling lies?" said my father, indicating the orange peel on the table. I lied about not lying, evidently, so as not to tell the truth: specifically, that I had lied about the apple. I didn't want the truth. I resisted it at all costs on every suitable occasion. For the concealment of secrets that were mysteries even to me, Father punished me with a strap.

I did have one adolescent enthusiasm, however, one which I certainly took conscious pains to keep secret from my parents. This was a passion for parades and festive processions, rallies and demonstrations. Especially, of course, demonstrations on Red Square. Officially, I could have got there by attaching myself, say, to a column of workers' representatives from my father's gramophone record factory. But Father, with his anti-Stalinist attitudes, contrived to avoid participation in such parades, deploying all manner of truths, untruths, and medical certificates. It was up to me and my friends, therefore, to get through to the bright future in Red Square Lenin-fashion—that is, under our own steam.

The city would be closed in every direction from Trubnaya Square, with all exits and side-streets cordoned off by police detachments: you could only get into Red Square if you were on the list. But we knew every interconnecting courtyard and every rooftop which permitted a leap over to the other side of the street; then along a wall linking two courtyards and you could reach a garage area, where only a set of cast iron gates divided you from the throng of demonstrators. At Marx Prospect, the official columns merged into a single festive procession: nobody checked the identity of demonstrators there and it was a simple matter to pretend you were the child of one of the participants at the other end of the column.

After our family's communal apartment, with its narrow corridors, closed doors, and whispering parents, after all that cupboard existence, was I not in search of space and anonymity in the endless variety of the faces—unfamiliar, but open and smiling—the paper flowers, the balloons, ribbons, and tinsel? The broad streets hummed with a chorus of voices, the squares echoed with the conversation of the columns, the yo-hoing of the amateur bands. Entry into Red Square was accompanied by the bravura clatter of heels on cobblestones and, floating above the voices, the sound of cheering and patriotic chorales from loudspeakers. Immediately beyond Minin and Pozharsky, brisk words of command came from the amplifiers, with the far-off baying of the demonstrators, as they saluted those on the Mausoleum rostrum in the distance. I struggled along in the scrum, as parents lifted children onto their shoulders. I could have been squashed flat in a moment, but I didn't realize that. After the atmosphere of invisible divination and ominous gestures, ambiguous hinting and doom-laden prophecies stretched out over those stifling family gatherings, I was intoxicated by the physicality, the thrusting swagger of this vulgar mystery, the asthmatic panting of the marching throng, with its smell of petrol and sweat, mignonette and *eau de cologne*. I wanted to be heard and move along with them all, just as long as they accepted me into that unfamilial kindred, that blended polyphony. Urged on by the roar of commands from the loudspeaker, the May sun rose on high, like a child's balloon, and began floating over the crowd like a mighty hurrah, accompanied by the guttural bellowing of the singing as it fluttered the banners above the sea of heads filling the whole of Red Square. My heart began thumping, a lump rose in my throat. This was exactly how I had envisaged life abroad from Aunt Irena's stories: a rich diversity of manners, dress, and faces. And yet, for me at that moment, how dismally wretched seemed the unearthly twittering of the beauty on the glossy record sleeve. Her abroadness seemed spurious: for me, Red Square was the *true* abroad.

I returned home sweat-soaked, radiantly clear-spirited and doubly secretive. I huddled in a corner, trying not to catch my father's eye. He circled as if sniffing me out, then took me by the chin and demanded: "Look me straight in the eyes. Admit it: you've been at that Stalinist orgy again?"

I gave it a try and said I'd been to the movies, but he answered that the cinemas were closed on days like this.

When all my fibbing versions were exhausted, Father proceeded to corporal punishment. For him, part of this was the public demonstration of my disgrace and humiliation. The door of our room was left ostentatiously open at such times. Once Aunt Irena stopped outside. "Undo your belt," ordered Father, "get your pants off." Retrieving them from the floor, he took the belt out: the instruments of torture were supplied by the victim. Father laid me out across the sofa and pulled down my shorts. At first what terrified me was not the beating itself, but my own nakedness. I wriggled about, trying to turn so as not to present my bare backside to the door, but father was wise to such tricks.

In a situation like this, the rare but brightly-etched moments of unspoken privacy and the intimacy of my relationship with Aunt Irena rose before me. But what humiliation, what sense of guilt was gnawing at her soul? My outward disgrace was plain to see. I lay, cheeks aflame, teeth clenched against the pain, flat out again on the settee in an ignominious pose. Resolving once to turn my head in her direction, I met her eyes, and read in them what until then had been unguessed: a sympathetic curiosity—or was it respect? We had achieved some ignoble equality through the secrets we preserved: she had her shameful secret, I had mine. We both hid the truth for family reasons and so both held the whole family in a state of tension. The revelation of her secret threatened to "scar me for life". My punishment convinced her, as I hoped, that I wasn't so easily scarred. The blows of the belt scorched me but I felt pleased rather than hurt: the whole scene had been a demonstration of my will power and endurance (the adolescent version of virility?), my ability to keep a secret. An odd smile played about her lips. I was pleased that she was watching me.

Her behavior had altered altogether by that time. Her former dress, the one which looked like a spectacle case, had been replaced by a nightgown: she used to let it hang loose and walked all over the flat in it, hardly noticing anyone around her. "You might wear a brassiere. For the child's sake," Mama would whisper to her. "Why?" Aunt Irena would reply, after some deliberation. "We are surrounded by nothing but lies and hypocrisy. Let him find out how things really are from an early age."

When the conversation at family gatherings turned to politics, nobody bothered to contradict her any more: Khrushchev's banging his shoe on the rostrum at the UN was replaced by the thunder of Soviet tanks across Eastern Europe. Her prophetic pessimism was being borne out. This struggle against the glossing-over of reality, however, did not extend as far as her hairdo. More and more often, through her half-open door, I saw her in front of the mirror, surrounded by vials and tins: with her little combs and brushes she would be tinting and powdering her head, by now greying, no doubt, from crown to chin. Tearing herself away from the mirror, she would take my face in her hands again and repeat: "Remember Solzhenitsyn's commandment: life without fibbing!" But she didn't mean the political situation in the country. Her face, which still seemed to me beyond compare in its golden crown of hair, was covered in droplets of perspiration and little pink spots. Or were they tiny pockmarks? Perhaps I had started to notice these spots and the network of wrinkles at her temple because I was growing up; just as I had also begun to notice that her nose was anything but Roman, and her lashes were nowhere near as dense and shady as the woodland paths of my childish imagination.

I felt sorry both for her and myself: because pity was beginning to take the place formerly held by adoration. Was my first apprehension of the dread of old age, the transformation of her hair's golden fleece into grey strands, the chief reason for my emigration? Or was I trying to break free of the family fetters which had sealed Aunt Irena's lips? In becoming an incorrigible liar in my own life, was not my leap across the Iron Curtain an attempt to set her a friendly example? And at the same time, rid her of the feeling of guilt and fear of scarring me for life.

In fact I failed to evade this lifelong scarring. What it boiled down to was that I couldn't get the image of Aunt Irena and her golden fleece, the golden foam of her hair, out of my mind. It didn't dawn on me at first. But how could it have been otherwise, if I had quitted Russia (forever, as it seemed back then), for the sake of that world which was associated most of all with her? And when I was composing those first letters to my parents in Moscow, it was her voice that dictated my own first impressions to me: "The endless variety of manners, dress, and faces. The abundance of consumer goods. A moveable feast. You sit with a cocktail at a café table and all this joyous, richly diverse world swirls about you. And you start to swirl with it." But Aunt Irena was not there for me to get up and begin twirling with her in this world, the way it was back then, when she used to rise from the table beyond the green lampshade, pick me up, and revolve to the unearthly purring from the gramophone. Not that I was all that depressed or lonely in this paradise, but the green lampshade, the gramophone, and the cascading serpentine locks of Aunt Irena in some waltz refrain kept recurring to my mind's eye more and more often. My lips would whisper, like those of Uncle Arkady: "And what about our Gorky Park?" Time and again I seemed to see the green lampshade and the gramophone, and the blue-grey smoke of the "Flowers of Herzegovina" lit up in a cloud above her golden crown; and she herself, a duchess, trying to convey to us mere mortals the unearthly words spinning from the record disc. It would seem that I was embodying her legacy: in real life I was living out the words of her dream.

At the time, however, she did not evince any particular enthusiasm for my plan to leave Russia for good. Emigration, she told me before my departure, should start from within: "You must first of all break open the dungeon of your mind, and only after that fling wide the Iron Curtain of state frontiers." What did she mean? What dungeons of the mind—and what secrets languished there in confinement? The simplest reason for my rejection revealed itself to me too late: fear. Fear at the revelation of Aunt Irena's dreadful secret, hidden in the dungeons of her mind. In Mama's view, I was afraid of being scarred for life. In actual fact, I lived in fear of discovering something monstrous about myself, something known only to Aunt Irena. I put on a show of hoping to get to the bottom of things and solving the riddle over there, beyond the magical Iron Curtain. Really, I fled so as not to come face to face with the truth.

Throughout all the subsequent years of my emigration, hints as to the existence of this truth arrived from my parents with enviable regularity. After seven years, the usual letter from Moscow reported rather obscurely that Aunt Irena had almost carried out her threat publicly, and had it not been for my mother's timely intervention, she would have perpetrated an outburst, so outrageously unseemly as to have disgraced our family in the eyes of all Moscow. The members of our family literally almost scratched one another's eyes out over this affair, despite Granddad's assurances that the source of the discord was exclusively to do with the stomach. Aunt Irena was temporarily hospitalized.

Whatever the reason, her unseemly outburst had taken place in my absence, and therefore could not concern me exclusively. But whom should it concern if not me? The more I racked my brains over this puzzle, the clearer I could picture her in the hospital ward, with the liver spots of old age, the pockmarks and parchment temples, her legendary curls faded and matted into dull strands. She was looking at me from the distance of the Russian present (now the inaccessible past as far as I was concerned) with her unblinking eye—the conscience of the age: as if to reproach me for deciding to change my habitation, rather than my mode of life, for swapping inner poverty for outward comfort, minus fears and secrets. A secret, as I've already said, is a pledge for the continuance of history, and as the experience of Aunt Irena taught me, it doesn't do to be in a hurry to reveal it: but the secret has to be yours and nobody else's. Other people's secrets, like other people's dreams, are of no interest to us. This nightmarish secret of mine, whose significance was unknown to me, remained back there, with her. After all, she might well lose her wits at any moment, or depart for the next world altogether, leaving me in the other next world of emigration without the least prospect of returning to the cherished plot of Russian history by way of this secret, which inspired me with such dread.

Any life to which there is no returning remains frozen for ever in our minds, and so when, after fifteen years, I received a letter personally from Aunt Irena, I sensed no lapse in time: it felt as if we had parted the day before. However, changes had begun to take place in the country since then, a metamorphosis not only puzzling to foreigners, but also to the citizens of the former Soviet state. "We have become exiles in our own country made unrecognizable by the tricks of history," wrote Aunt Irena, in English for some reason. It had never occurred to me that she knew English. Could that mystical lady from the glossy depths of the gramophone record have sung to me in those magical days of my childhood in the very language which, by the decree of history, had become my second native tongue? Was it for that reason I had chosen England as my second homeland: seeking, as it were, the echo of those sounds I had cherished since childhood for their arcane significance? Or had she calculated that I was so anglicized as to have forgotten my Russian?

"In Moscow, you'll feel quite at home politically speaking: we're all émigré anti-Soviets nowadays," she went on. "Since there are no longer external political divisions between us, we can forget about the geography of the country and concentrate on the geography of the mind. If, of course, you still love your aunty, and want to know the truth." In fact, this was the furthest thing from my mind: for me, the truth was that Aunt Irena had again begun to appear in my nostalgic dreams, as before in an aureole of fiery auburn hair, a low-cut watered-silk dress, high-heeled shoes, patterned stockings— my inaccessible Russia. *Irena, now I fling my heart to thee— catch it as I gladly bow the knee!*

After so many years of separation, the geography I had known had indeed been stripped away, like old wallpaper from the rooms of the family home: instead of the monument to Dzerzhinsky in the middle of my favorite square, there stood a docked stump of pedestal. Signs with pre-revolutionary street names had been nailed up all over the place, nominal symbols of the past seeming to the new Russia a firm pledge of the future.

My childish secrets under the glass pane were gone. There were no parades on Red Square, no penetration of police cordons, no thrill of the chase after stray cats. I had arrived at a moment of silent mourning, during my own wake. Moscow resembled a burgled apartment: all the nooks and crannies are as you remember them, but the rooms are bare and intruders' footprints are everywhere. I was apprehensive that my family past would be the same—plundered. However, my parents' hearth remained as it had been: from the smell of herring and boiled potatoes, to the green lampshade above the fringed brocade tablecloth—above all, in that same auburn treasure trove of curls, Aunt Irena's golden fleece of hair. I couldn't believe my eyes. I don't mean that I naturally expected to see an old woman with ashen rat's tails. As far as effect went, this was something stronger than dyed hair. She wore her low-cut watered-silk dress, its cut picked up by her rounded knee, and the instep of her shoe, accentuated by the stiletto heel. It was as if the years had passed, not in ageing, but in the discovery of her former self. It was as if what had happened to her and the country had been repeating Wilde's story of Dorian Gray: no sooner did Soviet power collapse, disfigured by decadence and ignominy, than my aunt's former charm, figure—panache as the English say, using the French word—came back to her. In high excitement at this meeting, I attempted to stammer out something about the old gramophone record, but nobody was listening to me now: after the initial embraces and distribution of presents, the oohs and ahs, the entire family immediately forgot about me and renewed their quarrelsome grappling over the future of Russia.

Uncle Arkady was the noisiest of them all. He was forever repeating the account of his time on the White House barricades during the putsch. For the umpteenth time, he offered his story of how the participants had formed a chain, arm in arm against the tanks, and when the general chant went up: "Svo-bo-da," those at the far end added: "BBC."

"*Svoboda,* you understand? *Liberty,* our American radio station," he elucidated for me, a foreigner.

"You honorable barricade participants have multiplied like the number of old Bolsheviks who toted logs with Lenin on voluntary Saturday labor," put in Aunt Irena; I got the positive impression that she had winked at me.

"You, Irena, are a confirmed cynic. During those three days, I learned to love and trust my own people," Uncle Arkady told her, his glance moist from his own moving account. His nostrils expanded, his double chin began to quiver and his asthmatic wheezing intensified. For the first time, perhaps, I witnessed the notorious parallel between revolutionary activity and sexual frustration: there was a physiological arousal in his political obsession, the more conspicuous for his advanced years. "When they hoisted our Russian flag at the rally, honestly, I could have wept tears of joy, like a child."

"Russian flag, indeed," Aunt Irena smiled wryly, addressing me confidentially in English, establishing a kind of conspiratorial relationship between the two of us. "They've hardly got one flag down before they put up another one. Are you going to put crosses instead of five-pointed stars? Are you wiping out the traces of your grubby little affairs in the so-recent Soviet past? They've taken that bronze Dzerzhinsky off his pedestal, but who's going to root him out of the minds of millions? Destroying monuments isn't combatting the grim past, Arkasha, it's vandalism."

"It's her stomach," said Father taking the place of my late Granddad, while Mama emulated my late grandmother by starting to distribute another portion of potted meat.

"And are they going to put a McDonald's in the Mausoleum?" Aunt Irena pushed her plate away, as if it contained Lenin's mummy. "And in place of Dzerzhinsky, Sakharov on a horse, is that it? They used to call Stalin the sunshine of our homeland, now they call Anna Akhmatova a newly discovered star. You think you can get rid of an unpleasant past by giving it a different name? It won't work! Freedom comes naked. The inner lie can only be destroyed by being totally exposed." Rising from her chair, she went to the window and began staring at her reflection as if actually contemplating pulling off her night clothes.

"She's off again. Nagging me hairless, forgive the pun." Uncle Arkady began trotting round the room, nervously clutching at his bald patch. Grey-haired and handsome Mama, who a moment before had been the presiding matron of the table, at once moved swiftly over to Aunt Irena. She hugged her like a first-year schoolgirl, and began babbling cajolingly: "Irunchik, I beg you. Think of the child." She glanced sideways at me.

Aunt Irena deftly stubbed out her *papirosa* in the ashtray with the view of the Kremlin. Her lips were clamped: "Are you on about childhood traumas again? This kiddy would have been a grandfather long ago if you hadn't instilled in him a fear of the female sex as personified in me." Knitting her brows purposefully she addressed me, to the general horror: "Do you practise onanism?" I flushed. "Do you masturbate over there in emigration?" she repeated, using the Latin root, as if to me as a newly-fledged Englishman the word masturbation was more comprehensible than onanism. Dumbstruck, I still went on smiling like an idiot. "Don't think I'm criticizing you for your bachelor activities. There's nothing to be ashamed of—masturbation helps to concentrate attention on one's own inner world. Apart from which, better masturbation than all these petty *amours,* shushing in corners, the hypocrisy of married life. For the sake of the children. To avoid scarring them. To depart from the truth. Children should be banned in Russia altogether! The most terrible actions of parents under the Soviets were for the benefit of the children."

"You know, Irka's right in a sense," said my father, addressing my mother plaintively, without raising his head. "She's right, but only to an extent of course. Bearing in mind our son's resulting penchant for lying. It's partly his stomach, I can't deny that."

"It's easy to reason like that, Mishunya, when you don't have the responsibility. She's never had a child. People who are childless should watch what they're saying," Mama flung back in answer, and at once clapped her hand to her mouth in fright. She'd obviously said rather too much.

"Did you hear that?" Aunt Irena said to me in English, in the infuriated voice of a private school matron. "Just you listen to her! And who sterilized my womb, made it barren and childless? Who visited this sterility, this childlessness, upon my head?"

"Upon your head or upon your womb?" I corrected her automatically, also in English.

"A good question indeed. Precisely," Aunt Irena went pale and looked at me with an ominous smile.

"Stop talking in English, as if nobody here can understand a word. I intended migrating to America too, incidentally. I took English classes as well, okay?" said Uncle Arkady, fidgeting on his chair and mopping his bald patch.

"I know what classes you took. With Mara in bed." Aunt Irena looked my mother up and down, eyes narrowed. "Of course, unlike me, you and your bald patch had nothing to lose." Edging fastidiously away from him, Aunt Irena shook her curls.

"What's my baldness got to do with anything?" muttered Uncle Arkady resentfully.

"I wonder what would you have looked like in my position? And what sort of a picture our wonderful Marochka would have made either?" Aunt Irena said, taking a puff at her *papirosa*.

"Nobody forced you to sleep with my husband!" Mother suddenly shrieked out, forgetting all my childhood traumas, as well as elementary decency.

"And who else should I sleep with while you were sleeping with my Arkady?" Aunt Irena shrugged, not a whit put out.

"I was absolutely alone," sniffed Mama. "You and Mikhail up to your fun and games on various official trips, pretending to us that you were travelling abroad. As if we didn't suspect anything. Mishenka working his guts out on far-flung assignments to feed his family, and you not least, the poor relation, with your idleness and philosophizing about East and West. He couldn't get a good night's sleep because of you."

"You should be grateful that it was me and not you that slept with your husband. With his long-distance musical assignments and the venereal diseases that went with them. Or were you ready to spend six months in the clinic instead of me?" said Aunt Irena.

"We wore ourselves out so that you needn't stint yourself after hospital," said Uncle Arkady. My mother, stately and grey-haired, rose from her chair and bore down on Aunt Irena, using her chest to pin her to the wall. Their faces radiated both malice and release: having finally come by the chance to insult one another openly, they sensed the weighty fetters of convention falling away, they could let themselves go. They seemed to have grown younger: their eyes flashed, their mouths hung half-open, like duelling pistols. Time seemed to recede by several decades, taking me back to adolescence, but with the difference that all the weird secrets of my elders were now revealed.

"And what do you think you're doing, basically, pretending you don't understand what this is all about, in principle?" My father had stayed silent in a corner up till this moment, but now addressed me with menacing exasperation. He had finally noticed me, an involuntary witness of this disgraceful family scene. I really didn't know what it was all about. "Do you mean to say that you've never heard anything of this?" I shook my head, my lips tight together. "But everybody knew about it!" he cried, banging his hand on the table, enjoining us to silence.

"But you all kept quiet about it," I brought out.

"We couldn't express in words what was obvious in any case, could we?" responded Aunt Irena from her corner.

"And you never heard, in principle, what the secret was, basically, that Aunt Irena kept from you all those years?"

I shrugged again, bewildered. In the menacing tone of his voice, my sensitive hearing could detect the panic of despair. But I had told him the truth: it had never occurred to me that anything of this sort could happen in our family—all these intrigues and adulteries. Intrigues, perhaps, yes, perfectly possible in principle, but adultery? "Do you believe him, Arkady?" my father turned to him.

"No, Mishuk, I don't. Do you, Marochka?" said Uncle Arkady. Along with the rest of my relatives, he was closing the ring around me.

"How can you believe such naiveté? It borders on cretinism. But my child can't possibly be a cretin," Mama proudly straightened up on her chair, chin high. "He was always a very receptive child, with healthy physiological reactions. I don't speak as a mother, but as a critical teacher. Even Irena can confirm that. Do you believe him, Irena?" She turned to her relative.

Aunt Irena shook her golden tiara. "Perhaps he was wholly preoccupied with his adolescent onanism and totally blind to the real world around him?" What I remembered was not onanism, but the Red Square parades and Father's belt, although it was too late to explain that now.

"Why tell lies?" sighed Father angrily, glaring at me, brows knitted, his hand reaching almost automatically for his belt—the habit of years gone by. Now he was going to ask me to drop my pants, stretch me out on the sofa, and lay into my bare backside with Aunt Irena looking on. A sweet-tasting lump, the accumulated tears of many years, grew in my throat. But this time I would hiss and scratch like that stray cat by the dustbins in the backyard of my childhood.

"Mikhail!" Aunt Irena stopped him with a queenly gesture. "Haven't the years of Stalinism cured you of the habit of resorting to violence when attempting to solve mental contradictions? Believe me, the best way to combat falsehood is not to go all out for the truth at whatever cost, but to expose the first cause of the lie. To lay bare the truth, you see? The naked truth speaks for itself," she said.

At that, as if to demonstrate the logic of her words, she performed an imperceptible gesture, like a circus conjurer. An instant before, it had seemed that everything was proceeding in a logical and decorous manner, when all of a sudden, something happened which had nothing to do with what had gone before. All I can remember is that Aunt Irena jerked her arm up to her temple, like a suicide with his pistol. Everyone leapt from their chairs, their hands also flying up towards her, rushing as if to save her from inevitable doom, but freezing into immobility, realizing that their belated efforts were all in vain.

I didn't actually apprehend at once what had happened. Mother uttered something between a short scream and a hysterical sob. An instant before, the former image of Aunt Irena had been swaying before me: she stood by the gramophone in the lacy aureole of her curls, in black décolletage with the smoke of "Flowers of Herzegovina" at her scarlet lips, as if shrouded in the mists of the past. A single movement of the arm and she had disappeared. My dream had disappeared— or rather, that which I had thought was my dream in my earlier existence. It was as if she had pulled up her dress and discarded her underpants before our eyes. She was demonstrating to us the naked truth. Her hand, its circus trick performed, lay limply along her hip: the aureole ripped from my past, the golden fleece of her luxuriant hair, was dangling from a fastidious finger. Not hair, to be accurate. Artificial hair. The auburn curls, sliding from her finger to the floor, resembled the pitiful pelt of some dead beast. A hairy little corpse was draped along the floor. It was a wig. All my former life I had been staring at a wig, lost in admiration of a dummy. I feared to lift my eyes and encounter the naked truth.

What had been hidden by the wig was more fearful than the revolutionary destruction, the Stalinist terror, and the Brezhnev stagnation. Above the gramophone hung an egg-shaped skull, its pink babyish bald spots covered here and there with tufts of grey hair, like dandelions. Grey strands stuck out over the ears, with an absurd pigtail, like that of some toy mandarin or a Don Cossack, secured by a hatpin on the top: it was evidently these pitiful remnants of vegetative cover that had held the wig in place. The nakedness of the scalp took something away from the powdered face with its heavily-penciled brows, its doll-like stick-on eyelashes, and the blood-red smudge of the mouth: it was as if this face, like the wig, did not belong to her either, but was held in place behind the ears with a safety pin, and could be ripped off and tossed into the dustbin. The denuded countenance threw into relief the puffy, gill-like cheeks, the coarsely-stitched wrinkled seam of the lips, the drooping purse of the Adam's apple, as well as the scared-rabbit expression in the old woman's swollen eyes. These eyes roved round the faces of her kin, searching for the admiring glance, anticipating congratulations and applause from a grateful public. Instead, I caught the sound of muffled sobbing, remarkably similar to the onset of vomiting. Father stood in a corner, pressing his face to the wall. Mother was rocking herself in her chair, head in hand. Uncle Arkady, eyes fixed on the floor, was soundlessly scratching the upholstery of his chair with crooked fingers. Of all those present, I alone had remained where I was, face to face with her.

"So then, it would seem there's nothing more to expose, whether in public or private life," sighed the bald creature, smiling serenely at me. "He," she said, pointing at me for the benefit of her dumbstruck relatives, "he will understand. The boy lives in a society where people are not ashamed of themselves. You do love me, don't you? Just as I am?"

Without waiting for an answer, she lit up her cherished "Flowers of Herzegovina" and began turning the handle of the gramophone. I was sure I could guess the words of the record. "Shall we dance?" she said, and held out her hand, looking me in the eye. It was the face of my Russia: unvarnished, without falsity or coy smirking.

"Cover yourself, do," I brought out at length, restraining a hysterical sob of my own. I bent down and retrieved the wig from the floor: "We can do without this truth of yours. We'll dance together one day. Only for heaven's sake, cover yourself up."

1992

Translated by Alan Myers

AFTERWORD:
ONE-WAY TICKET

You step outside your house for a breath of fresh air. After a while, you want to get back in, but you can't—you locked yourself out. It is not your home any longer.

Or, alternatively, you step outside your house to find out what's going on in the neighborhood. When you get back, you find its interior has changed beyond recognition. It is not your home any longer.

Or, yet again, you step outside your house to meet other people. By the time you get back you have changed beyond recognition so that everyone inside the house regards you as an alien. It is not your home any longer.

There are as many reasons for emigration from Russia as there are causes for suicide, and both are fatal. But, unlike the suicide, the émigré doesn't know what he is doing, and from the very moment of his departure starts plotting his triumphant comeback. Unlike the suicide, the émigré is not aware that his act brings him equally to that land from which no traveler returns.

In this sense, I am not an émigré. That is, I am not someone who dreams of returning to his homeland—if not today then tomorrow, if not tomorrow then next year. However, since I still write my novels in Russian, my literary persona dwells in a different location from the place of my actual residence.

Even today, twenty years after my departure, at every social gathering I always wait for the inevitable, cliché-ridden question—when, why, and how did I leave Russia, and do I intend to go back? There is a subconscious tendency in people to define strangers by their ethnic origin, and strangers in turn resent this attitude with a passion similar to that of children who resent remarks about their resemblance to their parents. In this war of stereotypes, I am on the side of the children: although I know now that it is impossible to rid ourselves of the past, it is exactly the attempt to do so that constitutes our sense of freedom and molds our personality.

I have a secret: Zinik is not my real name. My family name is Gluzberg. Zinik was a nickname from childhood which has been passed on, by word of mouth, from relatives to friends, until it finally crept into my passport as my second name. In the late 1960s, then a minor *samizdat* author, I started to use it as a literary pseudonym. Since then, it has become a token symbol of my second nature: literary activity was then, and still partly is regarded as a sacred and mysterious occupation in Russia. It is also identical in my mind with my Russian youth, so that with emigration from Russia in 1975, these two names began to represent two different ages of mine, two aspects of time in my life which existed simultaneously—one of the natural ageing process, the other, that connected with the name Zinik, with fictional age, with my literary *alter ego*. As all my published novels have been written since my departure from Russia, this second age of mine is associated with my émigré persona, which is the one of permanent youth—because the self-perception of an émigré is forever frozen in time, tied up with the moment of his fateful departure.

This doubleness of my name is only one example of the duality of my dubious character, and might serve as yet another psychological reason for my decision to leave Russia—except for the fact that there were quite a few people in Russia at the time who had second names or pseudonyms, and who never for a moment considered emigration. And there were as many other aspects of my Soviet past which might have prompted my decision to emigrate—the KGB, my Jewish origins, too many simultaneous love affairs, censorship, the unavailability of good beer and whisky, fear of the mob, and harsh winters. The list could easily be extended.

On the other hand, the reasons for *not* leaving were as numerous. I was lucky to grow up in a Russia which had shaken off her Stalinist nightmare. The corrupted servants of Brezhnev's empire wouldn't have survived in the harsher ideological climate of the old terror, and they allowed others some space in which to breathe freely. Unless you were in open confrontation with the authorities, you could, in a freakish way, enjoy the life of the big and boisterous city that was Moscow. With plenty of state money still around, the arts scene allowed quite a few diversions from the Party's general line. My older peers and mentors who used to frequent the Café Artistique opposite the Moscow Arts Theater would talk about Paris and London without ever having been there, and quote Joyce and Huxley as if they were next-door neighbors. It was a bizarre version of café society in a prison-like city. Life was only enhanced by the proverbial Russian warmth of closely knitted relationships within a tight clan of friends, the sense of chosenness of belonging to the spectacular Russian spiritual history, and the prominent place which the writer occupies in the Russian psyche. All this made the old fear—of finding oneself outside the proximity of Russia—more acute than ever, and the decision to emigrate more precarious.

No one in his right mind leaves his own country unless he is forced to do so. I wasn't forced to leave Russia: I must then either have not been in my right mind, or ceased to regard Russia as my own country. Or both. To appreciate the sheer irrationality of emigration from such an evil prison-like empire as Brezhnev's Russia seemed to be, you have to stop using political criteria and Aristotelian logic. In fact, for every rational reason to break away from the Soviet regime there could be found an equally powerful opposite argument in favor of remaining in your native land. There was no other way to treat the dilemma but to accept that a step such as emigration sets you beyond the boundaries of rational reasoning. In the case of Soviet Russia of the 1970s, the boundaries of rationality were identical in my mind with the Soviet borders.

Disabused of the Soviet utopian ideas, as I eventually was, I would still even now regard my Soviet past as a part of my present psyche. Soviet Russia was not just a country: it was a civilization, a religion, an indelible part of one's nature. Like every Soviet citizen of that time, I couldn't comprehend my existence outside Russia; at the same time, I was obsessed, as everyone else (and I mean *everyone*) was, by a desire to find out how it would feel to be completely severed from her by the Iron Curtain. I wanted to be inside and outside at one and the same time, to belong and not to belong, to be and not to be. This last paradoxical answer to Hamlet's question is probably the most faithful definition of the émigré state of mind.

Russians have always looked for their identity outside the confines of their national history: they invited the Vikings to conduct their state affairs for them, they turned to the Greeks of Byzantium for their religion. To be a foreigner has always been a precarious but covetous privilege in Russia. I was a Russian Jew, and apart from everything else this ethnic definition implied, it meant, then and there, that I had a chance to avoid the common lot of remaining forever a Soviet prisoner. In fact, as the Moscow saying went in the 1970s, "Jewishness is not an ethnic origin, but a means of transport." Anyone who could substantiate a claim of having a distant uncle abroad was able to apply officially for an exit visa on the grounds of "reunification with relatives in the West", often leaving a real family behind in the Soviet Union in doing so. In the 1970s, thanks to Western political pressure for the opening of the Soviet Union's borders, such visas were in many cases granted by the government. On the other hand, there were—and still are—many Russians of Jewish descent who would never dream of considering such a move. All of us, up to a point, considered ourselves predominantly Soviet in origin.

My father was a communist, and I never heard a word of the Jewish language spoken at home. The only notion of God which I ever came across in my youth, besides the theology of Marxism-Leninism, was drawn from ancient Greek mythology which, in an ironical twist of the country's educational system, was much encouraged in Soviet schools. These myths were probably the underlying cause of the duality of our consciousness with regard to the outside world. There was the biblical sense of guilt associated with departure from the motherland and induced by the Party doctrinists of the utopian Soviet state; this sense of guilt, however, existed in our consciousness alongside the urge to follow Ulysses' example in his quest for the Golden Fleece in distant lands. And our objective view of the world beyond was always an ambiguous one: separated from the rest of Europe not only by the self-erected Iron Curtain but also by her Slavic cousins, Russia developed an acute inferiority complex towards Europe. An adoration for the enlightened civilization was in the Russian mind always mixed with a censorial contempt for the corrupted Western universe.

Back in the 1970s, while I was collecting the necessary documents for my exit visa application, the Soviet cultural bureaucrats with whom I came into contact kept warning me of my doomed future as a writer in a foreign land, telling me how I would wither away without everyday contact with my native speech, deprived of the inspirational influence of the great Russian culture. They presented to me an image of life in the

West as that of a man marooned on a desert island, with no records, no radio, no newspapers, no friends, only savages prattling in an incomprehensible lingo. Strangely enough, some of my first acquaintances in Britain were members of the "chattering classes", who equally tried to convince me that there was no chance for me to survive in a cultural desert such as England, that life in the arts could only be found across the Channel and beyond, possibly even only back in Russia. That is, their opinion of England was not very much different from that of their counterparts in the Soviet Union.

They didn't know that, for a writer, there is no such thing as good or bad experience, a good or bad country. Every experience is either absorbed by the writer into his prose, or not—that is all. The artist can create beauty even in the most depressing surroundings. Like history itself, the writer's eye makes no distinction between the greatness of victory and the humiliation of failure.

Somerset Maugham, in his novel *Cakes and Ale,* puts into the mouth of his hero a remark about Henry James, who "turned his back on one of the great events in the world's history, the rise of the United States, in order to report tittle-tattle at tea parties in English country houses. . . . Poor Henry, he's spending eternity wandering round and round a stately park and the fence is just too high to peep over, and they're having tea just too far away for him to hear what the countess is saying." Though the tone is highly ironical, the passage's disparaging character is illusory. In fact, bearing in mind that Maugham himself was frequently attacked by his contemporaries for his own lack of social commitment, it could be one of the exercises in self-derision of which Maugham was so fond. He calls James's attitude *il gran refiuto,* and he implies that in literature there is no such thing as an insignificant matter and that the writer, in order to achieve his artistic greatness, should sometimes deliberately avoid the great themes.

This was of some consolation to me in moments of despair when I was ready to curse myself for giving up my part in the great drama of Russian history, for exchanging it for the life of the émigré—one neither in full possession of his past nor able to embrace his present, discontented with his host country and bitter about the one he has left behind, whose existence is riddled with a sense of guilt for betrayal of his own ideals, whose only defense is haughty disdain and self-derision, who is on a perpetual search for a scapegoat for his own misery. This is the stuff the émigré's dreams are made of, while it is from this stuff that the writer in exile must create.

I was told many times how demoralized and petty England had become when she was stripped of her imperial past, how Englishmen hated ideas, how philistine was their attitude to the arts. Not to mention other notorious national characteristics such as xenophobia and love for animals, frigidity, homosexuality, and soccer violence among both sexes. Some people with whom I talked even believed that these characteristics were uniquely English. But even if this were true, people forget that, when it comes to summing up the essence of a given national temperament, there is always an *opposite*. Orderly and petty bourgeois as England sometimes looked, the country was also the cradle of world anarchism, the arena of the most daring manifestations of sexual liberation, the battlefield of the most extreme ideological confrontations.

Anyway, in the everyday contact of real life, one usually has to deal with the exceptions rather than the generalizations, and, in my own experience, I have rarely come across such openness, generosity, warmth, kindness, gregariousness of character, and sense of loyalty among human beings as in England.

Still, false or not, even generalizations can strike a power-ful chord in the writer's imagination. The fertile ground for the writer is that where, underneath an ostensibly alien sur-face, he recognizes familiar features; when the chaos of alien sounds finds, in some strange way, an echo with something that had previously existed only in his consciousness. The Russian émigré mind, hungry for parallels to its own mon-strous experiences, finds intriguing similarities, speculative and far-fetched as they might appear, between, say, the émigré's separation from his homeland and that of the Angli-can church from Rome. The historical isolation from the West and separatist tendencies in Russian society could find a sym-pathetic ear in England among those who fear total assimila-tion into Europe. The émigré's suspicious and cautious at-titude towards new life is quite comparable to that of the islander to foreigners. Even the old colonial instinct which urged Englishmen abroad to rediscover their ancestors' expe-rience in a foreign land is not dissimilar to that of the émigré, an empire builder in his own right, if you like, who is forging different connections in different parts of the world populated with his old cronies alongside foreign compatriots. The émi-gré world is as illusory as Prospero's island. How could there be any shortage of parallels in the land of Shakespeare and Dickens, writers who never fail to provide us with any range of possible, and impossible, manifestations of human nature?

To provoke your imagination, however, such parallelisms should come to your mind in an unpredictable fashion. Hav-ing been mad enough to leave my native country, I didn't want any artificial substitute for my motherland of the kind to be found, say, in the warm familiarity of Israel, fed by wave after wave of East European immigrants. I wanted to settle down in a place which would be as alien as possible to my Soviet past, in order to discover in myself things I would not be made aware of if I had stayed among familiar faces. No other country in the world is as unlike Russia as England: in the eyes of the British islander, all foreigners are ex-Isles, and I was one of many. England deprived me of the false sense of being the chosen one, deeply ingrained in the minds of all Russians, most of whom never traveled abroad.

England successfully undermined my Russian belief in political ideology as a ruling passion in one's life. England taught me to cherish the difference rather than the unity of ideas. England trained me to get on with the job at hand regardless of the opinion of others, without constantly seeking signs of encouragement or disapproval in somebody else's eyes. England taught me the old Christian truth that one should try and isolate the evil, for it to die out, rather than fight it and thus be contaminated by it. England reassured me in my Chekhovian belief that the neglected details of mundane life could play the most crucial role in artistic creation.

This collection of stories is a kind of travelogue—one which begins with a narrator, a Jewish Muscovite, visiting Kiev, and ends with him, now a Russian Brit, visiting Moscow twenty years later. This long route should be seen not so much as a spiritual journey in search of a new identity, but rather as a compelling way of shedding one's false self-images. The stories have one common denominator: they are all about a presumptuous man whose preconceived ideas are shattered by an unexpected turn of events. We think that we are guided to the Holy Land by the calling of our ancestors, while in fact we are driven there by the urge for sexual gratification. We think we are simply falling out with our best friend, while in fact we are on the threshold of religious revelation. We think our life is ruled by ideas, while in fact we are controlled by baser instincts. We think that we are victims of some petty ideological manipulation, while in fact we are passionate creatures who indulge in a most bizarre play of desires. The narrator of these stories emerges from each such episode with a new sense of puzzlement and consternation. He may consider himself smart, but his self-indulgent posturing is undermined by the sheer unpredictability of human folly and obsessions, itself the best weapon against the omniscience of the authoritarian mind.

Most of the stories in this collection were conceived in the late 1980s and early 1990s, when we were confronted with the imminent collapse of the Soviet system—a turn of events which I, in my blind pessimism, had never believed would take place. Having witnessed at that time a number of accidental encounters between old émigrés and their former compatriots visiting the West for the first time, I was made aware that my attitude to my former circle of friends and comrades-in-pens back in Russia was changing and had to be revised once again.

In the 1970s, my decision to emigrate from Russia was partly a gesture of defiance: I wanted to show that the dictates of political geography, tangible in the form of the Iron Curtain, were irrelevant to the survival of Russian literature, of the spiritual life of the nation in general (whose best authors were published abroad, anyway). My first attempt at that émigré theme, relatively new to Russian letters, could be dated to the first years of my voluntary exile when, involuntarily separated from my wife—she couldn't join me at the time of my departure, a fact which eventually led to four years of separation—I began an intensive correspondence with friends in Moscow, trying to describe my foreign experience not as an outsider, not as a Russian visitor abroad, but as a participant in a strange new life who was searching for a new vocabulary to describe things which had never existed in his native tongue.

It was then that, for the first time, I became aware of the weird aspects of émigré existence. With the vanishing of the hope that you will ever meet your correspondent again, and what with the delays and censorship of letters, the interrupted telephone calls from abroad and the unexpected messages from your closed-off ones delivered through foreign visitors, the sense of time and space becomes distorted as in a Gothic novel, where the ghost-like existence of the main characters is defined by the Iron Curtain which separates them from the real world. Gothic or not in character, any fatal departure from the familiar territory for a distant shore creates the illusion in which your past life becomes like the outlines of the plot of a ready-made novel—and emigration itself a literary device.

The sensation of weirdness was not dispelled when the eerie faces of former Soviet citizens started to turn up in Moscow after twenty years of absence. The reunification of old friends was not entirely cordial. The hero's welcome was followed immediately by a tendency to square accounts and acrimonious reciprocal accusations of forgetfulness and lack of understanding of each others' sufferings. Before the fall of the Iron Curtain, I and my circle of readers had been united by our mutual past and our current opposition to the system. We shared our present—in words, if not geographically.

Nowadays, when the old country has slipped from under the feet of its citizens, it is as if the whole population of the Soviet Union itself has emigrated—beyond the Iron Curtain, into a strange land of freedom and uncertainty. People do not recognize their own present, trying in vain to reconcile it with the Soviet past. I and my potential readers are now on equal footing, but we have emigrated into different countries—they, into the future of Russia, and I into England's present. And never the twain will meet?

Freud pointed to our mother's womb as the starting point on the journey into exile. Marx would have mentioned the alienation of labor. For a Christian, it all started with Adam's false step and fall from paradise; for a Buddhist, it is the attempt of the soul to become independent of the body. For those of us who believe neither in paradise nor in the existence of the soul, it is an attempt to step out of one's own self, to see oneself from the outside, beyond the looking glass. We are not trees: instead of roots stuck in our native soil, we have legs on our bodies and thoughts in our heads—hence our ability for spiritual travels. Unlike material objects, we can become alien to our own natures. In that sense, life is a permanent emigration: from past to present, from this world to another, from a wife to a lover, from life to death. The fact that the characters of these stories could be defined as émigrés in a political sense, only serves here as a dramatic device to highlight the wider conflict between divine inspirations and human limitations. The process of ageing is perhaps the most effective literary device ever imaginable.

I can indeed say now that I have emigrated from the country to which no traveler returns. The Soviet borders opened, the dungeons crumbled, and I ceased to be an outcast. With the demolition of the Iron Curtain, the émigré is being transformed into the expatriate; as an author I have been transformed into a vassal of the literary metropolis. A man who is left in the wilderness without a compass will always wander in circles. For a writer there is, and always will be, only one way to liberate himself from this vicious circle of invisible confinement: to write a new work, to create a new style. Maybe that is why I have written this confession in English, not in my native Russian.

London, December 1994.

DATE DUE